The Thore Sisters Series

Ink & Iron

Silk & Silence

Pleasure & Prose

Lessons & Leather

Hana York
Pink Pop Publishing

The Thorne Sister Series

(Books 1-4)

Copyright © 2025 by Hana York

All rights reserved.

www.HanaYork.com

Contents

Ink & Iron

A steamy small-town romance about a guarded veteran, a bold tattoo artist, and the ink that sparks something real.

Hana York

Pink Pop Publishing

Ink & Iron

(The Thorne Sisters Book 1)

Copyright © 2025 by Hana York

www.HanaYork.com

Contents

Prologue

LOLA

Mornings in Briar Hill smelled like coffee, motor oil, and gossip.

I propped the studio door open with a cinderblock I'd spray-painted black and gold, the edges still crusted with glitter from a Thorne sisters' DIY night gone sideways. It let in the breeze—and, sure enough, the scent of cinnamon rolls from Sweet Brew next door came drifting in like temptation wrapped in sugar.

Needle & Ink was quiet for now. Just the hum of my ancient tattoo machine warming up, the faint flicker of fluorescent light over the front desk, and the ghost of last night's playlist still echoing in the back of my head. This was my favorite time of day before the buzz. Before the pain and stories and secrets people etched into their skin like armor.

I wiped down my station for the third time. It didn't need it. I just needed to move.

Vivian texted twice already: Bring wine or don't bother showing up.

We had dinner plans at her place tonight—me, Eliza, Veronica, and Vivian. We were sisters by blood, bruises, or both. We didn't always agree, but we showed up, especially when Eliza cooked.

Vivian would bring the fire, Veronica the sarcasm. Eliza would bring heart-shaped napkins or something equally earnest.

And me? I'd show up with a bottle of red and pretend I wasn't the one who needed it the most.

The bell above the door jingled.

I looked up—and saw him.

Big. Broad. Shoulders like a wrecking ball. A jaw that had clenched its way through more than one war, if I had to guess. Dark eyes. Scar peeking from under the sleeve of a plain black tee.

He stepped inside like the world weighed too much.

And something in me leaned toward him before I could stop it.

Chapter One

TANNER

I almost turned around twice.

Once when I saw the sign—Needle & Ink scrawled across the glass in thick, stylized lettering like it dared you to walk through the door. And once when I saw her behind the counter.

She didn't look up at first. Just kept wiping down the same corner of her station with the kind of focus you only have when you're trying not to think too hard. Ink-stained fingers. Dark hair knotted on top of her head. Tank top. Tattoos up one arm and down the other.

She looked like every reason I shouldn't be here.

I stepped inside anyway.

The bell overhead jingled. She looked up. And for a second—just a beat too long—her eyes landed on me and stuck.

Something flickered across her face. Surprise. Curiosity. Heat?

Then she blinked, and it was gone. "You lost?" she asked, voice smooth, slightly amused. Like she already knew I wasn't the walk-in type.

I cleared my throat. "No. I was referred. A buddy of mine, Sam Bell. You did a piece for him a few months back."

Her eyes narrowed a little, but her mouth tugged into something that might've been a smile. "Forearm phoenix?"

I nodded.

She set the rag down, finally giving me her full attention—and that was a problem. Because now I couldn't stop looking. Or thinking about how long it had been since someone looked at me like that. Sharp. Like she was trying to figure out where I broke.

Her gaze dropped to my arm—the thick scar that curved down my arm and beneath my bicep, old and ugly, raised and pale against my skin.

She didn't flinch.

Didn't ask what happened.

Didn't pretend not to notice, either.

"I'm Tanner."

She nodded once. "Lola."

A beat passed between us—quiet, full of things neither of us said.

I cleared my throat. "Can you make it disappear?"

She stepped forward, slow and sure.

"No," she said. "But I can make it mean something else."

I should've left after that.

That would've been the smart move—turn around, say thanks but no thanks, and find a way to live with the thing carved into my skin.

But I didn't move.

I just stood there like some idiot who didn't know how to carry his own pain. Like I was waiting for her to tell me what to do with it.

Her eyes flicked back up to mine, steady and unreadable. "Do you have a design in mind?"

I shook my head. "No. Just know I don't want to see it anymore."

She nodded again as if that made perfect sense. "You want to book a consult or just talk now?"

Now. Before I lost the nerve.

"Now's fine."

She gestured toward her chair. "Sit."

It wasn't a request. It wasn't rude, either. Just... matter-of-fact. Like she already knew I'd listen.

I sat.

The chair hissed under my weight, the leather cracked and worn from use. The studio smelled like antiseptic, old ink, and something warm and clean, like citrus and cedar. Her, maybe.

She moved quietly around me, grabbing a sketchpad and pencil. Every motion efficient, precise. No small talk. No pity. Just focus.

I tried not to stare. I failed.

There was something about her—some mix of stillness and heat that didn't make sense.

"I won't ask what happened," she said without looking up, pencil moving fast over the page. "But if you want the design to mean something, I need to know what kind of story you're trying to rewrite."

Her voice was quiet. Nonthreatening.

Still hit like a sucker punch.

I didn't answer.

But I didn't get up, either.

LOLA

He didn't talk.

That didn't surprise me.

What surprised me was that he stayed.

Most guys with that kind of scar—military bearing, thousand-yard stare, whole body held like it's bracing for an impact that already happened—they don't sit. They ghost. They cancel. They postpone.

But not this one. Tanner.

He sat down like he didn't know why he was doing it, just that something told him he should.

And God help me, I noticed everything.

Not just the scar. The *man*.

The way he moved—deliberate and stiff, like his body wasn't entirely his. The cut of his jaw under that scruff. The thick forearms that flexed when he crossed them like he was holding himself in place. The long, quiet breath he took when he looked around my studio.

And yeah, fine, he was hot in that *haunted, ex-soldier, too-broad-for-this-chair* kind of way. But it wasn't just that. It was the way he looked at me, like he wasn't used to being seen. Not like that. Not like a person.

I knew that feeling.

I picked up a pencil and gave my hands something to do before they did something reckless. Like touch him.

"I won't ask what happened," I said, eyes on the sketchpad. "But if you want the design to mean something, I need to know what kind of story you're trying to rewrite."

He didn't answer. Didn't leave, either. That was something.

I kept sketching—lines, shapes, movement. Nothing permanent yet. Just breathing space between us.

But my pulse had already picked up. And it wasn't just professional curiosity.

This man was carrying a war inside him.

And for the first time in a long time, I wanted to help someone put themselves back together.

Even if it meant breaking my own rules.

I didn't usually let clients rattle me.

They came in with their heartbreak, their grief, their declarations of rebellion. I gave them ink and shape and permanence. That was the deal. I didn't carry it. I translated it.

But Tanner sat in my chair like he didn't know how to stop hurting.

And I hated how much I wanted to be the one to stop the hurt.

He didn't fidget. Didn't scroll his phone. Didn't fill the silence with nervous chatter like most people did when they were afraid to be alone with themselves.

He just... watched.

I liked that he didn't pretend. Didn't fake ease or flirt. He was just raw and quiet and *there*. And the air between us felt like it was holding its breath.

I added a curve to the shoulder of the design, something that would trace the edge of the scar without trying to erase it. I could feel his gaze on my hands—not in a creepy way, but just... aware. Present.

"What kind of thing are you thinking?" he asked finally, voice low and rough. Like he hadn't used it in a while.

I glanced up, our eyes meeting for half a second too long.

"Something that fits," I said, my voice steady despite my stomach having other ideas. "Not something that hides."

He nodded once. Said nothing else.

But he didn't look away, either.

And I couldn't decide if I wanted to draw faster just to get him out of here—or slower, so he'd stay.

Chapter Two

TANNER

S he didn't rush.

That was the first thing I noticed.

Most people get uncomfortable in silence. They talk. Fill it with noise or bullshit or questions they don't really want answered.

But Lola just... let it be quiet. Let me breathe.

And still, somehow, I couldn't.

I watched her work, the way her fingers moved—steady, confident, stained with ink. There was a softness under the edge like she'd built armor around something breakable and dared the world to try her.

And God, I shouldn't have been thinking about her fingers.

Or her mouth.

Or the curve of her back as she leaned over the sketch-pad.

I wasn't here for that.

I was here because I hadn't slept through the night in months. Because every time I looked at that scar, I saw the moment I didn't save him. And because some idiot friend of mine said she was good at turning shit into art.

He didn't mention she looked like that.

Didn't say I'd feel something just being in the same room.

I didn't like it.

Didn't like how I wanted her to keep talking, even though every word scraped at nerves I thought I'd buried.

"What kind of thing are you thinking?" I asked because I needed to say something, anything before I did something even dumber—like ask if I could see her tattoos up close.

She looked up. And Jesus.

It was just a glance. A flick of dark eyes, sharp and knowing. But it hit like a punch to the ribs.

"Something that fits," she said. "Not something that hides."

I swallowed. Nodded. Said nothing.

But I didn't move.

I wouldn't. Not until she put something over that scar.

Maybe not even after.

She angled the sketchpad toward me. Not a complete design—just the bones. Shape. Flow.

A tree. Twisted. Weathered. But still standing.

Branches reaching upward. Roots sinking deep. One half inked in heavy black lines, the other lighter, almost like it had been sketched and half erased.

"It's just an idea," she said, watching my face. "I can change it. Or scrap it entirely."

I stared at it longer than I meant to.

It shouldn't have hit me like that.

But it did.

"It's..." I cleared my throat. "Yeah."

Yeah.

That was all I could give her.

Because *saying* what it meant—admitting what it reminded me of, what that scar stood for—would've cracked something I wasn't ready to face in front of a woman who looked at me like she already saw too much.

"You sure?" she asked, voice gentler this time.

"No," I said honestly. "But I think it's the first thing that hasn't made me want to walk out of a room in a while."

She didn't smile. But something softened in her eyes.

"Alright," she said, tearing the sheet off and setting it aside. "I'll refine the lines and pull together some options. Come back tomorrow, and we'll get started."

I nodded and stood.

She moved closer to grab something off the counter, and for a second, we were side by side—close enough that I could smell the citrus in her shampoo and feel the warmth radiating off her skin.

She didn't look at me.

I didn't look at her.

But it felt like we both noticed.

"Same time?" I asked, already at the door.

She didn't turn around.

"Same time."

LOLA

Vivian opened the door in stilettos and a silk robe as if she wasn't hosting three sisters and a bubbling lasagna.

It was Vivian's apartment, but Eliza had taken over the kitchen—because Vivian didn't cook. Takeout was her art form. The only reason her oven had seen anything more ambitious than reheated Pad Thai was because Eliza treated it like her own.

"Wine?" she asked, already walking away.

I held up the bottle I brought. "Way ahead of you."

Veronica was camped out on the couch, legs tucked under her, sipping red and pretending she wasn't critiquing the entire room's energy. Eliza popped out of the kitchen wearing an apron with dancing eggplants.

"Dinner's almost ready!" she said with the kind of sunny cheer that made me want to check for hidden Xanax.

I handed her the wine, dropped onto the nearest chair, and kicked off my boots. "You know, normal people eat in clothes they can stain."

Vivian flicked a hand. "Normal people are boring. And I'm not the one wielding marinara."

Veronica arched a brow. "That's true love. Silk robe near red sauce? Risky."

Vivian winked. "I like to live dangerously."

We all laughed, and for a moment, the room felt easy—like the years of damage, drama, and tangled father-based trauma didn't hang between us like old smoke.

Then Eliza set down a bowl of garlic knots and turned her too-bright smile on me.

"So," she said. "Anything new at the shop?"

I stabbed a knot with my fork. "A guy came in today."

Three sets of eyebrows lifted in unison.

Veronica leaned forward. "Tattoo client or tall, dark, broody mistake?"

I shrugged, keeping my face neutral. "Tattoo client. Big. Quiet. Ex-military, I think."

Vivian's eyes gleamed. "Oooh. The strong-silent-'will-definitely-ruin-you-in-bed' type?"

"Viv," Eliza scolded, cheeks pink.

I didn't answer.

Which was probably answer enough.

We finished off two bottles of wine, the pan of lasagna, and half a tiramisu Eliza insisted was "experimental," which meant she'd tried a new recipe and immediately regretted it.

Vivian kicked us out around nine with a dramatic yawn and a vague threat about needing her beauty sleep. Veronica stayed behind—ostensibly to help clean up, but probably just to snoop through Vivian's beauty products.

They were twins—Vivian and Veronica. Identical in face, but that's where the similarities ended. Vivian was all fire and flair, born to be onstage. Veronica didn't need volume—she could silence a room with one eyebrow and a better vocabulary. Calm, composed, and secretly the most dangerous of all of us.

Eliza hugged me a little too tightly at the door. "You okay?"

"Course," I said. "Just full of wine and sibling judgment."

She didn't buy it, but she let me go.

***

When I got home, my apartment above the shop was quiet. It still smelled faintly of ink and lemon oil. I kicked off my boots, stripped to a tank and shorts, and sat on the edge of my bed without turning the lights on.

I didn't usually bring clients home in my head. I left them at the shop with the needles, ink, and stories they didn't want to carry alone.

But Tanner had followed me here.

The way he sat so still. Like he didn't trust his body anymore. The way he looked at me—guarded, wary, but watching. Like he needed something and hated that he did.

Like I was a risk he hadn't decided to take.

And damn it, he'd gotten under my skin faster than any man had in a long time.

I wasn't thinking about his scar.

I was thinking about his mouth. His hands. The weight of him in that chair and how my pulse had spiked every time he leaned forward.

He was coming back tomorrow.

I should've been focused on the design. The lines. The meaning.

Instead, I lay back on the bed, stared at the ceiling, and whispered to the dark:

"Don't be stupid, Lola."

Chapter Three

LOLA

The shop was too quiet.

Which was ridiculous because I liked it quiet in the mornings. The hum of the machines. The scent of antiseptic and eucalyptus cleaner. The creak of the old floorboards beneath my boots. Usually, it settled me.

Today, it didn't.

I'd already rearranged my ink trays twice, restocked the disposable razors, and changed the liner in the sharps container—none of which were urgent, and all of which I was doing just to keep my hands busy.

Because he was coming back.

I hadn't even touched him yet—hadn't so much as wiped down the scar—but he was already under my skin.

I didn't know what I expected. Maybe that he'd ghost. That he'd let whatever pulled him in yesterday get swallowed by whatever made him bolt in the first place.

But he'd booked the appointment. Said he'd be back.

And it was almost time.

I rechecked the clock like that would make him materialize.

The bell over the door jingled.

I didn't flinch.

But my pulse sure as hell did.

He stepped inside, still all shadows and silence. Same black T-shirt, different jeans. Hair damp like he'd just showered. Clean-shaven. Or clean-ish. The scruff had a purpose now.

And the minute our eyes met, I knew I was screwed.

Because it wasn't just attraction. It was something more profound. Like recognition. Like my bones already knew him.

"Morning," I said, nodding toward him.

"Let's do it," he said.

And just like that, I forgot what peace had ever felt like.

I nodded toward the back room. "We'll work in the private suite. Better lighting."

And fewer eyes. Not that there were any this early, but I didn't need the front windows catching me staring at this man like I hadn't seen muscles before.

He followed without a word, boots solid against the wood. I could feel him behind me, heavy presence, silent intensity. It did things to me I didn't have names for.

Inside, I gestured to the chair. "Shirt off."

He hesitated—not out of modesty. No, this was something else. A breath. A brace. Like shedding a layer wasn't just fabric—it was armor.

But then he did it.

And I had to focus on keeping my professional face when all I wanted to do was stare.

The scar was even more brutal under the fluorescent lights. It was pale and raised, jagged in places, old but angry, and surrounded by muscle that was very much not angry—just... distracting.

I pulled on gloves. "I'm going to clean the area first. Let me know if anything's uncomfortable."

"Already is," he muttered, but there wasn't bite in it.

I stepped closer, cotton pad in hand, antiseptic in the other. Pressed gently to his skin. He didn't move or flinch, but his jaw flexed just once, sharp and silent.

I told myself I was studying the canvas, mapping the lines, and focusing on how the ink would wrap around the damage.

But my hand lingered. Just a beat too long.

"You tense like you expect it to hurt," I said, soft.

"Doesn't?"

"Not yet."

He glanced down, eyes catching mine. "You always get this close?"

I lifted a brow. "Only when I'm working."

And then I turned back to the tray because if I didn't, I would have done something really unprofessional.

Like find out how that tension tasted.

TANNER

I'd taken a hit to the ribs on a mission once. Cracked clean through. Breathing felt like fire for weeks.

This?

This was worse.

Not because it hurt—but because it didn't.

Her hands were steady. Gloved. Clinical. But I felt it straight through the bone every time she touched me.

Her hands moved over the scar like it didn't intimidate her.

Like she wasn't afraid of what it meant or what it might still hold.

Most people either stared too long or pretended not to see it. She did neither. She just worked with a calm that made it hard to breathe.

She was standing close enough that I could smell her shampoo again—citrus and something clean. No perfume. No drama. Just her. Simple. Real.

I couldn't remember the last time someone touched me without flinching first. Without a clipboard in hand. Without checking for wounds or measuring damage. Just touch—warm and unguarded.

"You tense like you expect it to hurt," she said quietly.

"Doesn't?"

"Not yet."

I looked down, caught her eyes, and regretted it instantly. Not because of what I saw—but because of what I felt. Like if I stayed in that moment too long, I'd unravel.

"You always get this close?" I asked, mostly because I needed something to say before I said something *stupid*.

She didn't blink. Just lifted one perfect brow. "Only when I'm working."

Then she turned away, and I was grateful—and disappointed.

Jesus. What the hell was wrong with me?

I should've been focused on the design. The lines. The damn scar.

Instead, I was thinking about her mouth.

About how she hadn't asked for my story but already felt like she knew it.

About how I wasn't sure I'd want to leave when this was over.

Which was the one thing I absolutely shouldn't want.

She returned with the stencil in one hand and a quiet focus in her eyes. The kind that said she'd already seen everything she needed to, even if I hadn't said a word.

"You good with black and grey?" she asked, voice back to business.

"Yeah. Color doesn't feel right."

"Didn't think it would."

She pressed the stencil gently to my skin, smoothing it over the scar with practiced fingers. I knew I was supposed to be paying attention to placement, but instead, I was counting her heartbeats by the rhythm in her touch.

"You always this quiet?" she asked, not looking at me.

"Depends."

"On what?"

"If I've got something to say."

That earned me a glance. Just a flicker of a smirk at the corner of her mouth.

"And here I thought you were brooding for the aesthetic."

"Do I look like a man who cares about aesthetics?"

Her gaze dropped to the stencil she'd just set, then back to me. "You came to a tattoo artist to cover a scar. So yeah. I'd say there's a little vanity in there."

That made me laugh—short, low, and unexpected.

She looked almost smug about it.

"What about you?" I asked. "You always this direct?"

"Only when I'm awake."

I shook my head, still smiling.

She wiped the stencil with a clean cloth, careful, focused. "You from around here?"

"No. Just passing through. A friend who lives nearby said I should come to see you."

"Right. Sam Bell."

"Yeah. He said you were good."

"Didn't say I was charming?"

I looked at her then—really looked.

"Figured that out on my own."

Chapter Four

LOLA

I'd been called many things—hot, intense, intimidating. "Charming" wasn't usually on the list. Not that I needed it to be.

I was joking when I said it.

But then he looked at me—quiet, steady, all heat and honesty—and said, *"Figured that out on my own."*

It wasn't a flirt. It wasn't even a line.

It was just true.

I covered it with a smirk. "Careful. You keep saying nice things; I might start to think you like me."

He didn't blink. "Would that be a problem?"

God.

His tone wasn't cocky. It wasn't defensive. It was just... honest. Steady. Like if he said it, he meant it. No armor. No pretense. Just him.

I cleared my throat and turned back to the machine. "Alright, let's get this going. Sit back and try not to flex. Not that I'm judging—it just makes my job harder when guys try to impress me mid-line."

"I'll try to behave," he said, and that damn voice of his did something warm and wrong to my insides.

I snapped on a fresh pair of gloves and rolled my stool closer. "This part might sting."

"I've had worse."

"Bet you have."

And then I pressed the machine to his skin, and the room went quiet except for the hum of the needle—and the space between us that felt anything but still.

The machine hummed steadily in my hand, low and familiar. Tanner didn't even blink when I hit the first stretch of scar tissue. Most guys twitched. Flinched. Tried to play it cool.

He just stayed still. Silent. Like he was used to pain showing up and sticking around.

"Guess I should've warned you—I talk when I work," I said lightly. "Occupational hazard."

"Yeah?"

"Yeah. Helps keep people from passing out. Or panicking. Or making me listen to their breakup playlists."

A hint of a smile tugged at the corner of his mouth. "No panic here."

"Mm. Strong silent type. Knew it."

I leaned in, focusing on the curve of the design. "I've got three sisters. We could fill a room with noise and still not get a word in edgewise."

He glanced at me. Not much, but enough.

"I'm guessing you didn't grow up with that kind of chaos," I said.

"No."

That was it. One syllable. But it didn't feel like a wall, more like a line drawn in the dirt, waiting to see if I'd cross it.

"Veronica owns a sex shop, Vivian runs a burlesque club, and Eliza teaches kindergarten. So, depending on who you ask, we're either empowering women, corrupting society, or overachieving in the baked goods department."

His brow lifted slightly. "And you?"

"I make art out of pain," I said, pressing gently over the ink. "You be the judge."

He was quiet for a second.

"Then I'm starting to think I came to the right place."

My hand didn't shake, but it was a near thing.

I didn't look up. Just kept the machine moving like my pulse hadn't just done something complicated.

TANNER

Lola talked while she worked. Just like she said she would.

Stories about past clients, all of them ridiculous. A guy who passed out and woke up flirting. A woman who cried because her tiny finger-heart wasn't "emotional enough."

The one that stuck with me was a bachelorette party that came in for matching peaches. One of them passed out halfway through and still swears hers is crooked.

"It's not," Lola had said. "Her left butt cheek just flexes weird when she laughs."

She'd said it with a straight face like it was just another Tuesday.

It should've been noise. A distraction.

But it worked.

Her voice kept me tethered—kept me from getting pulled under by the sound of the needle and the weight of everything behind it.

I didn't mean to say anything.

But somewhere between a story about a guy who wanted a skull made out of kittens and how her fingers shifted over the curve of my arm, it just... slipped out.

"I almost didn't come in."

She didn't miss a beat. "Why?"

I kept my eyes forward. "Because the last time I tried to cover it, I made it as far as the stencil before I walked out."

She didn't say anything.

Just let me keep going.

"I got the scar the day I lost someone. A brother in every way but blood. I carried him out, but it wasn't enough. Hasn't felt like enough since."

Her machine didn't slow. Her hands didn't hesitate.

But her voice went quieter. "You're not the first person to walk in here trying to make peace with something like that."

I finally looked at her.

"Maybe not, but you're the first person who made me think that might actually be possible."

She looked up.

I saw the truth in her eyes.

Then she said, "Not everything painful needs to be erased. Some things deserve to become something new."

She didn't say anything else. Just turned back to the piece and finished the last few lines with a kind of focus that didn't feel clinical anymore.

It felt personal.

When she finally pulled the machine away and peeled off her gloves, the hum in the room faded, but something else lingered. Something quieter. Heavier.

"That's it for today," she said, voice low. "We'll let it settle and finish the shading tomorrow."

I nodded, even though I wasn't ready to move. My arm felt warm and raw but steady. Like something had shifted under the skin—and not just the ink.

She reached for the bandage and paused like she was about to say something else. Then didn't. Just wrapped the area with practiced care, her fingers brushing the inside of my wrist.

She didn't ask if I was okay.

Didn't tell me I'd be fine.

She just looked up and said, "Same time?"

"Yeah," I said. "I'll be here."

I pulled my shirt back on, rolled my shoulder, and reached the door before turning back.

"You don't talk just to fill silence," I said.

Her brow lifted.

"You talk so people don't disappear into it."

She held my gaze and gave a single, deliberate nod. Nothing more—but it was enough.

Chapter Five

LOLA

I was in trouble.

Deep, dangerous, "don't say I didn't warn you" kind of trouble.

Not that I'd admit it. Not even to my sisters. Especially not to my sisters.

He came back.

Honest, intense, makes-me-want-to-break-my-own-rules Tanner. And I was doing an even worse job of keeping him out of my head than yesterday.

"Same time?" I'd asked, trying not to sound eager.

"Yeah," he said. "I'll be here."

And damn it, I couldn't stop thinking about the way he said it—like he'd already decided this meant something.

I should've been thrilled. This was what I did. What I loved. People brought me their scars—physical and otherwise—and let me help them turn pain into art. But Tanner wasn't just another client, and we both knew it.

The smart thing would've been to keep my distance. To focus on the design and pretend like hell he wasn't getting under my skin so fast it might as well have been permanent ink.

Instead, here I was, watching the clock and feeling like a teenager waiting for her first crush to call.

Get it together, Lola.

I had two hours before he showed up again, which was plenty of time to pull myself together and remember how to be a professional.

Instead, I spent those two hours picking up the phone twice before finally calling Veronica.

"Pleasure & Co.," she answered. "How can I—"

"Hey, it's me."

"Ugh, you ruined my customer service voice. What's up?"

"You free?"

"I can be. Vivian said you were acting weird at dinner last night."

I rolled my eyes even though she couldn't see it. "Thanks, spy twins."

"So? Was she right?"

I sighed. "Meet me at Sweet Brew in ten?"

"Ten it is."

She hung up before I could change my mind.

Veronica was already at a table when I got there, drinking what looked like half coffee, half cream. She arched a brow as I slid into the seat across from her.

"You seem surprisingly on edge for a woman who got laid last night."

"I didn't," I said, stealing a sip of her drink.

"Didn't get laid? Or didn't do anything to make you this twitchy?"

"Both."

"Huh." She watched me over the rim of her mug. "Then why do you look like you've been staring at your phone all morning, waiting for a guy to text?"

"Because he's coming back, and I can't get him out of my head," I said, hating how it sounded. "I need you to talk some sense into me."

Veronica's lips curved into a slow, knowing smile. "Tell me everything."

I filled her in—Tanner walking in like a storm cloud, his honesty, his silence, the way he made my pulse forget every rule I'd set for myself.

When I finally shut up long enough to breathe, Veronica just shook her head. "You're screwed."

"Gee that's comforting."

"You want comfort? Talk to Eliza." She leaned closer. "You want the truth? You're fighting a losing battle and loving every second of it."

"I don't love anything about this," I said, but my voice lacked conviction.

She gave me a look that said she wasn't buying it. "Lola, you've been walking around with an emotional chastity belt ever since—"

"Don't."

"Fine. Since your last 'adventure.' But this guy? He sounds different. You said it yourself—he's not just another client."

She was right, and it killed me.

I'd let one man get too close before. Watched him walk away because I wouldn't let my walls come down fast enough for him.

"I don't do this, Vee."

"Maybe you should," she said, tone gentle but unyielding.

I didn't answer.

TANNER

When I needed to clear my head, I ran.

Always had. Miles of nothing but breath and blood and grit between me and the things I didn't want to think about.

Today, it didn't work.

I pounded down the side streets around my place, gravel crunching under my sneakers, lungs burning — but every time I thought I could outrun it, there she was.

Lola.

Sharp smile. Quick hands. Those wild, steady eyes that made me feel like maybe I wasn't broken past fixing after all.

I slowed to a walk, dragging a hand over my face, breath misting in the early morning air.

Goddamn it.

This wasn't supposed to happen. A tattoo. A cover-up. That was it. Not...whatever the hell was happening now.

I pulled out my phone without thinking, scrolling to Sam Bell's name. The guy who sent me to Needles & Ink in the first place. The guy who, apparently, had been holding out.

He picked up on the second ring. "Bell."

"It's me," I said, still catching my breath. "You got a second?"

"For you? Always. What's up?"

"You could've warned me."

There was a beat of silence. Then, a knowing laugh. "Let me guess. You met Lola."

"Yeah." I kicked a rock off the path, watching it skitter into the gutter. "She's...fire."

"Told you she was the best."

"That's not what I meant," I muttered.

Another laugh. "Buddy, if I'd told you the truth, you would've chickened out."

"Maybe," I admitted. "Or maybe I just would've prepared better."

There was a pause, longer this time.

"You good?" Sam asked, tone shifting.

I stared down the empty street, the pulse in my chest not all from the run anymore. "Yeah. Just...wasn't expecting this."

"What, feeling something that doesn't suck?"

I huffed out a laugh despite myself. "Something like that."

Sam's voice softened. "Look, man. You've been carrying that weight for a long time. You deserve something good. Don't fuck it up by overthinking it."

"Wasn't planning to."

"Good." Another pause. "She's one of the good ones, Tanner. Careful with her."

I nodded, even though he couldn't see me. "I know."

We hung up, and I stood there for a long minute, feeling the weight of the conversation settle in my chest.

Careful with her.

Yeah.

But something told me I wasn't the only one who needed someone to be careful.

I jogged the last few blocks back to my place, showered fast, changed, and sat on the edge of my bed, lacing up my boots.

Same time, she'd said.

I'd be there.

And this time, I wasn't just showing up for the ink.

I was showing up for her.

For whatever this was.For whatever it could be.

No walls. No halfway.Not this time.

Chapter Six

LOLA

I wasn't great at sitting still. Never had been.

But after meeting Veronica for coffee and getting a pep talk disguised as a verbal smackdown, I found myself back at the shop, staring at the clock like a lovesick idiot.

Tanner wouldn't be here for another hour.

I grabbed my sketchpad, flipping past a few half-finished designs, and started to draw. Something simple. Clean lines. Maybe a floral wrap or a geometric pattern. Something that didn't make me think about broad shoulders, quiet, steady hands, or a mouth that could ruin a girl with a single look.

I was halfway through a rough design when I realized I'd started sketching a pair of sharp, clear, intense eyes.

Tanner's eyes.

I muttered a curse under my breath and flipped the page, trying to shake him out of my head.

The phone buzzed across the table.

I grabbed it without thinking, half-hoping it was him. Instead: Eliza.

I smiled, even as a tiny knot of worry formed in my gut. Eliza didn't call in the middle of a workday unless something was wrong.

I answered immediately. "Hey, sunshine. Who do I need to take out?"

There was a sniff on the other end of the line. "No one. I'm fine."

Liar.

I straightened in my chair, all pretense of sketching forgotten. "Talk to me, Eliza."

She let out a shaky breath. "It's stupid."

"It's never stupid if it's making you feel like this."

Another breath. "One of the moms at school. She... she said I was too young to understand real responsibility. That being 'cute' isn't the same as being capable."

I felt my blood pressure spike immediately.

"Eliza—" I started, already planning a full-scale take-down.

"I know," she said quickly. "I know it doesn't matter. I know it's just one person's opinion. But it got under my skin, you know?"

Yeah. I knew.

People saw what they wanted to see, especially with someone like Eliza—bright, sweet, open Eliza—who wore her heart on her sleeve and didn't realize how fragile it could sometimes be.

I leaned back in the chair, pressing a hand over my eyes.

"You are responsible as hell, and you're more capable than half the jackasses walking around this town," I said fiercely. "That woman's just jealous because you've got a heart and a brain, and she's got a minivan and a superiority complex."

Eliza let out a watery laugh.

I smiled, but it twisted a little in my chest.

Because for all the teasing and chaos between us, Eliza was *ours*.

Technically, she had a different mom—the one Dad left ours for. But it had never mattered—not once. She was our sister in every way that counted; anyone who made her feel like she was less could catch hands.

"You're good, Eliza," I said, voice low. "Better than most people deserve. Don't let one bitter woman make you forget that."

There was a soft sniff. "Thanks, Lola."

"Anytime. You want me to come down there and glare at her until she cries?"

She laughed, a little stronger this time. "Maybe later."

"Good. Because I have a client coming in soon, and I need to pretend I'm a respectable business owner for at least another hour."

"You are a respectable business owner."

I grinned. "Don't tell anyone. I've got a reputation to maintain."

We hung up a few minutes later, and I set the phone down, staring at the wall.

It was funny, the lines we drew around ourselves. The walls we built. We thought they kept us safe.

But sometimes they just kept the wrong people out.

The bell over the door jingled, and I looked up.

Tanner stepped inside—solid and steady, like he belonged there—and smiled at me in a way that made my heart do something reckless and stupid.

Yeah.

Maybe it was time to stop hiding behind the walls.

Maybe it was time to see what could happen if I let someone in.

Really let them in.

TANNER

I wasn't restless. Not anymore. The run had burned off the worst of it—the sharp edges, the confusion, the instinct to bolt when something felt too real.

But it hadn't burned out the part of me that wanted her.

That part felt stronger than ever.

So instead of pacing circles around my life like I usually did when shit got complicated, I found myself pulling open the door to Needle & Ink like it wasn't even a decision anymore.

Like it was inevitable.

She looked up when I stepped inside—and damn.

One look at her, sitting there like a storm I wanted to walk into, and every excuse I'd ever used to keep people at arm's length went up in smoke.

The music was different today. It had a slow bass line and a steady drum. It matched the beat in my chest—all anticipation, hunger, and need.

"Right on time," she said, voice smooth as the track spinning through the speakers.

"Hope you haven't been staring at the clock."

"Don't flatter yourself," she said, but a spark in her eyes made me think maybe she had. At least once.

Then she smiled, small but real, and it knocked the breath out of me all over again.

"You ready?" she asked, nodding toward the back room.

Was I? Hell no. But that didn't stop me from following her.

I wasn't ready. Not for the way she'd slipped under my skin without a needle. And definitely not for the way I wanted more of whatever this was—more of her. She hadn't turned on the overhead lights, just a warm lamp in the corner that gave the room a quieter, more intimate feel. The kind of light that didn't hide anything but didn't blast it into view, either.

"Shirt off," she said, already snapping on gloves.

I hesitated again. Not because I minded stripping down—but because every time I did, it felt like letting her see more than I knew how to cover. But then I did it. And I saw something in her eyes that made it worth the risk. It wasn't pity. It wasn't shock, sympathy, or any other reactions I hated. It was understanding. Like she knew what else came off with that shirt—and liked me better for it.

She rolled closer, machine in hand. "You look tense."

"Been that way a while," I said.

"Doesn't have to stay that way." She smiled—full this time, bright and unguarded—and it did more damage than any needle. Made me want to lean in, like a moth to a flame with no sense of self-preservation.

I just shook my head and watched her work.

She hit the first line and didn't bother with distraction. Didn't talk. Just focused on the design taking shape on my arm, on the scar. Like she knew, the only thing that kept me here was her—her hands, her eyes, her silence.

"Thought you said you talk when you work," I said finally, missing the sound of her voice.

She scooted closer, gaze never leaving the ink. "Only when people need it."

Her knee brushed mine. Not an accident. Not an apology. Just contact. And that was almost worse than anything she could've said.

"You think I don't?" I asked quietly.

She didn't answer right away.

Didn't look up.

But when she spoke, her voice was soft and sure. "I think you're stronger than you let yourself believe."

And there it was—that feeling again. Like she saw through every defense I'd ever put up and knew exactly who I was underneath.

"Guess that makes one of us," I said finally.

The needle kept going, but her hands were gentle. Careful. Like she knew she was leaving more than ink behind.

We didn't talk after that. Didn't need to. There was something better than words between us—something real and raw, like the lines weaving their way across my skin. It felt different this time. Less like covering a wound and more like letting it breathe.

When she finished, she peeled off her gloves and drew back just enough for air to find its way between us again. But not enough for me to feel like it had really returned.

"Same time tomorrow?" she asked, pulling the bandage tight.

I nodded. "You know it."

"See you, Tanner."

I went to the door without looking back. If I had, if I'd seen the way she watched me go, I might've stayed. Given in to whatever the hell this was pulling so tight between us. But I made it outside—back into the daylight and air that didn't smell like her—before letting out a breath I didn't know I'd been holding.

And that's when I saw the sky.

Going dark, low, and sudden. The kind of storm that hit fast and hard, unexpected as a sniper round.

I cursed under my breath and headed for my truck in long, deliberate strides.

I'd make it out ahead of the worst of it.

Get back to the rental. Let my head clear.

Maybe even convince myself this thing with Lola—this reckless want that felt more dangerous than anything else—wasn't going to happen.

But then my damn truck wouldn't start.

I sat in the driver's seat for longer than I should've, fingers flexing on the steering wheel like they could squeeze life back into an engine that wouldn't turned over.

Raindrops pelted against the windshield.

Harder. Louder.

A crack of thunder split the air, too close to ignore.

I didn't want to walk back in there. Didn't want her to see me stranded or helpless. But the storm had other plans.

With a half-sighed curse, I got out and headed back inside.

Chapter Seven

LOLA

I was cleaning up, trying not to think about how his voice sounded when he said, "You know it," when the bell over the door jingled again.

He stepped inside, wet around the edges and looking like a storm just tried to kill him.

For a second, I thought he'd changed his mind. That he was coming back to finish what we'd barely started letting ourselves want. But then I saw the set of his shoulders, how his jaw flexed once and held.

"Truck's dead," he said, shaking rain from his hair. "Mind if I wait out the worst of it?"

I didn't flinch, but my pulse did. "Sure. No problem."

His eyes met mine—dark, searching. Like he hadn't expected me to say yes.

"Really," I said. "It's fine." Then, because I couldn't help myself: "You look like you could use a drink."

He hesitated again, like accepting anything more would be more complicated than just sitting through a storm.

But then he nodded. "Wouldn't say no."

I went to the back and grabbed a couple of beers from the mini fridge, heart thudding in my chest like it knew exactly how close I was to trouble.

"Not fancy," I said, extending one as I came out.

He took it and followed me to the back of the shop where I kept a beat-up leather couch for clients who needed more time than I could give them in the chair.

"Didn't peg you for a beer drinker," he said, settling in at the other end.

"First mistake," I said, cracking mine open and trying not to look like I was cataloging every single way he'd gotten under my skin.

Another crack of thunder split the sky, shaking the windows.

"You weren't kidding about it getting worse," he said, glancing outside.

"No," I said. "This might be the kind of storm that hangs around for a while."

A pause. A single breath suspended between us.

"Guess I'm not going anywhere soon," he said, voice low.

I should've nodded. Laughed it off. Said something that shut this down before we got in any deeper than we already were.

Instead, I took a long pull from my beer and smiled like I knew exactly how much trouble I was courting. "Guess not."

We sat silently for a few minutes, the rain pounding harder now—insistent, unrelenting. Like it was determined to soak everything in its path.

"You got a lot of these?" he asked, gesturing to the walls where sketches were pinned like memories.

"A few." I shrugged. "I get bored easily."

Something flickered across his face—a mix of surprise and curiosity.

"What?" I asked, taking a sip.

"Never met anyone like you," he said.

And there it was again. The honesty hit like a gut punch. I should've deflected. Should've said something sarcastic.

Instead, I heard myself say, "Good."

I didn't usually do this—didn't let clients linger or let myself care what they said when—but Tanner was different. He made me want things I wasn't supposed to want. He made me feel reckless.

And God help me. I liked it more than I should've.

Something low and rough moved through his throat. Almost a laugh. Almost a sound he didn't let himself make. I felt it under my skin, even if he didn't let it out.

"You don't pull punches, do you?" he asked.

I shook my head. "Not my style."

"Yeah," he said, a fire lighting behind those dark eyes. "I can see that."

And then we just sat there, beer in hand, listening to the storm rumble and boom like it had something to prove. There was too much space between us and not enough at the same time. My pulse was doing things I couldn't control.

He took a long drink and tipped his head back against the couch, eyes closed for half a second before he looked at me again.

"You ever done this before?" he asked.

"What?"

"Let someone hang around like this."

"No," I said honestly.

It didn't faze him. He didn't ask why I was letting him now—maybe because he already knew the answer or perhaps because it was easier not to say it out loud. I should've been trying to hide how much I wanted him there, but instead, I wondered what would happen if I let myself want more.

I watched him from under my lashes, heart racing. He looked good there—too damn good. Like he belonged on that old leather couch more than any client ever had. Like maybe I'd been waiting for him to show up all along.

The rain pounded harder, and everything inside me surged toward him—reckless, hungry, breaking every rule I'd set for myself.

"Want another drink?" I asked, even though he had barely touched the first.

His eyes held mine, steady and full of things we weren't saying. "Sure."

He got up before I could move, covering the distance to the mini fridge in a few long strides that reminded me just how much space he took up and how little room I had left to pretend this was anything but inevitable.

He handed me another bottle without a word and sat back down closer this time. My pulse kicked hard against my ribs.

TANNER

God, she was beautiful.

Not in a way that was easy or delicate. She was all sharp angles and inked lines. Edges that looked like they should've been hard but weren't.

The rain pounded the windows, louder now, like it needed us to hear it over anything else. But I didn't care what was happening outside the shop—I only cared about what was happening inside it.

She was so close I could feel the heat coming off her skin. I was so drawn in I wasn't trying to stop it.

"I don't usually do this," she said again as if she needed me to know what kind of risk she was taking.

I took a long pull from my beer, then set it on the table without breaking her gaze. "Neither do I."

And then I kissed her.

Leaned in slow enough for her to back off if she wanted—but God, she didn't—and kissed her with everything I hadn't let myself feel until now.

She tasted like beer and something sweet and dangerous. Like everything I'd been trying to keep at arm's length since I walked into this place. Her lips were soft, tentative at first—like she couldn't believe we were doing this—but then they parted, and there was nothing tentative about it anymore.

Her hands found their way to my hair, pulling me closer, and that was it. I was gone.

This was reckless. Stupid.

Perfect.

We broke apart just long enough for her to breathe, "You're sure about this?"

I didn't hesitate. "No." Then kissed her again, deeper this time. "Yeah."

She pulled back, laughing a little against my mouth. Low and throaty, a sound I wanted to hear again and again.

"We're in so much trouble," she whispered.

"Good," I said, echoing her from earlier.

And damn if I didn't want to find out just how deep we could get.

It was addictive, the way she leaned into me. The way she took what she wanted without hesitation. The way it felt like we were going up in flames and neither of us cared how this burned. Before I knew what was happening, I had her underneath me on that old leather couch, the weight of my body pressing down on hers, and nothing but a whisper between our mouths. This was insane. Reckless. Everything I shouldn't want. But Jesus, I did. And from the way she wrapped her legs around me, pulling me closer until there was no space left between us, she wanted it too.

I kissed her neck, her shoulder, the line of ink that ran up her collarbone. She arched against me, fingers digging into my back like she needed to hold on or get swept under.

"Lola," I said, voice rough. "We—"

She cut me off with another kiss.

"Don't think," she whispered against my mouth. "Not right now."

Her hands slipped under the hem of my shirt, and I almost lost it. It felt good.

She pulled the shirt over my head in one quick motion, and everything else went with it.

The need for distance, for control. For anything but her.

The feel of her skin against mine was all heat and madness. Then she kissed me again. Harder. Deeper. Like we'd both been starving for this and finally got brave enough to admit it.

Her touch moved over me—fingers tracing muscle, scar, everything I thought I'd have to protect—and didn't flinch from any of it. The raw honesty in the way she took me in almost gutted me. It didn't matter we were on an old leather couch with rain hammering down around us—it felt like the only place I wanted to be.

I shifted, rolling her on top of me, loving the weight of her body pressing down on mine. She paused a second, propped up on one arm, eyes searching my face like she needed to be sure this was happening.

"You're different," she said quietly.

And before I could answer—before I could tell her how she made me feel more alive than I had since that day in the desert—she pulled her tank top over her head.

And God, if the sight of her didn't make my heart stop. Ink and skin, all fire and vulnerability. I pulled her down to me, kissing her like I'd die if I didn't.

Chapter Eight

LOLA

I'd forgotten how this felt. Not just the physical—his weight, his heat—but everything else. The way desire tangled with fear and excitement until you couldn't tell them apart. Recklessness. Want. All those things I'd built walls around and pretended didn't matter. Tanner's hands moved over me like he needed to memorize every inch of skin he touched. His scars pressed against mine made me forget which were his and which were inked into me by something other than an artist's needle. We were making out like teenagers on my studio couch, rain pounding at the windows like a wild percussion line, and I didn't want any of it to stop.

I kissed my way down, slow and deliberate. Felt him shudder underneath me when I reached the waistband of his jeans. God, I hadn't done this in years— hadn't wanted someone like this—and how much I needed him was heady and terrifying. How much it felt like I'd never stop needing him if I let this happen.

He was watching me with an intensity that burned away everything else. Watching like he couldn't believe I was really doing this.

I opened his fly and felt the tension in him coil so tight it almost unraveled me. Then he was free, hard, and ready, and my pulse was racing so fast I could feel it pulse in my neck.

"Lola," he said, a warning, a plea.

But I didn't stop. I took my time kissing up his cock before taking him into my mouth fully and letting myself taste just how much he wanted this.

I lowered my head and took him in inch by inch. My name became a groan on his lips. It made me bolder. Made me reckless. Made me want to give him everything he hadn't let himself feel until now.

"Jesus," he whispered, voice raw and unsteady.

And then he stopped talking altogether.

I took him deeper again, moving with a rhythm that matched the storm outside—steady and wild. His hips bucked once, sharp against me. He didn't have to say how close he was—I could feel how every muscle in his body strained for something more.

And God help me, when he let go, it was better than anything I'd imagined.

It took a while for his breathing to steady. For the tension and heat to unwind into something that felt like relief. I lay on top of him, tracing the line of ink that ran up his shoulder, feeling the aftermath ripple through him. Felt him catch my hand and pull it to his mouth, kissing the inside of my wrist like he needed to make sure I was still real. Still there. Like he didn't know I was already so far gone for him, I'd never find my way back. "Tanner," I said softly, unsure what would come out after his name but needing to say it anyway.

He rolled me onto my back with the kind of care that made everything inside me twist tight again, then kissed me so slow and deep it almost wasn't a kiss anymore. Almost something else. Something dangerous and terrifying in all the ways I hadn't let anything be since—

Don't think, Lola.

But even my voice couldn't drown out the thought that maybe this time would be different.

Maybe this time, the risk would be worth it.

"Beautiful," he said, voice rough and honest.

He undid the button of my jeans, tugged them off in one swift motion, and growled when he saw how wet I was.

The first stroke of his tongue sent a shockwave through me—hot, electric, obliterating every other sensation until all I could do was dig my fingers into his hair.

"Tanner," I said, breathless. Desperate. "Oh God."

The way he took me apart was all skill and chaos. He kissed like he meant it—like he wasn't afraid of what would happen if we burned out too fast or fell too far.

The first wave hit me hard—sharp, unstoppable—as he pressed two fingers inside. He didn't slow down, didn't back off. Just kept going until I was arching against his mouth, gasping his name like it was the only thing left to say. My body arched and shuddered around him, pleasure spinning almost out of control until he brought it crashing perfectly down.

"Jesus," I breathed. "I—"

Before I could finish, he brought his lips back to mine and kissed me through the aftershocks until it felt like I was still coming. Like every nerve ending in my body had gotten lost and didn't want to find its way back.

He pulled away just enough so I could see the fire in his eyes. The heat and purpose and need that could've scared the hell out of me if it hadn't felt so damn good.

We stayed like that for a while, hearts pounding in a rhythm neither of us tried to fight.

I moved first, kissing his shoulder—soft, quick, easy—like I could convince myself this was casual. He pulled me closer until I wasn't sure where he ended, and I began.

"So much trouble," I whispered again.

He shifted so we were face to face, our bodies lined up with nothing between them but heat and a million uncertainties.

"Good," he said softly, like it was the only answer that fit.

TANNER

I shifted, pulling her into my lap. The weight of her on top of me felt like the first easy breath I'd taken in years. I didn't want to let go. Didn't want to think about what happened when this storm passed or how much harder it would be to walk away once the rain stopped and we both remembered who we were. Instead, I just pulled her closer.

She smiled at me, a reckless, unguarded thing that squeezed through my chest.

There was something raw and exhilarating about having her like this, looking right at me with all that fire and intensity.

"You're impossible," she said, tilting her head like she couldn't believe this was real.

"Not yet," I said. "But give me time."

She laughed, low and throaty, and it did something wild to me. Made me want more.

She moved against me, her bare skin slick with sweat, and the noise in my head went silent. Like everything I carried had been set down for a moment. Like I could finally breathe.

I kissed her again—slow, deep, unhurried—and let my hands drift to the curve of her back. She was beautiful above me, hair wild and eyes dark with want.

"I don't usually do this," she said again, but this time it was breathless. Hungry.

"Neither do I," I echoed against her mouth.

"Got anything?" she asked, voice low and edged with need.

I nodded, breathless. "Yeah. Hang on."

The last time I'd been with someone... hell, it was long enough that I couldn't remember—but I wasn't unprepared. I reached for my jeans, found my wallet, and pulled out the foil packet.

She watched me unwrap it, eyes hot and intent on every move I made. I rolled it on with hands that didn't feel like mine, too eager, too unsteady.

She didn't wait—just shifted over me, sliding down in one slick motion that almost undid me before we even started.

"Fuck," I groaned, every muscle tightening as I watched her take me in.

I caught her hips and thrust up hard, and her cry matched mine in a way that undid me completely.

God. I wrapped an arm around her back and held her steady as she moved against me—easy at first, then faster—fingernails dragging down my shoulder and leaving marks that felt better than anything I'd ever known.

"Lola," I said, rough. Desperate.

Her name was the only thing I could manage.

The only thing I wanted to say. She rode me harder, head thrown back like she didn't care if she broke us both. Her breath came fast and shallow, matching mine.

With every thrust, with every movement of her body, I felt myself getting closer to the edge. She was wild above me, untamed and unrestrained, and it was the most beautiful thing I'd ever seen.

I wasn't going to last.

Neither was she.

She reached between us and touched herself in a way that almost finished me right there. "Close," she said, voice tight and wild and everything I needed to hear. Her fingers moved faster, and I was right there with her.

And when we crashed over the edge together, it was chaos. She shattered around me, pulsing and clenching and saying my name like a damn prayer. I exploded into white heat and perfect oblivion, her name a hoarse shout as everything shattered around us. Perfect and brutal and everything I needed it to be.

I didn't know how long we stayed like that—the storm pounding outside, our bodies tangled and slick with sweat and desire. Long enough for my heart to stop racing. For hers to slow against my chest.

Long enough for me to wish this moment would never end.

I hadn't meant for this.

But damn if it wasn't perfect.

I held her there, arms tight around her back, wondering how the hell I ended up on a couch with a woman who was supposed to be nothing but ink. Supposed to be safe. Instead, she was everything.

I didn't want to think about leaving.

"Lola," I started, but she shifted and cut me off with a kiss.

"Don't say it."

I laughed against her mouth, feeling lighter than I had in years. "You don't even know what I was going to say."

She pulled back just enough to see my face, hair falling wild over her eyes. "Doesn't matter." There was something vulnerable in how she looked at me—unguarded and terrifying in all the best ways.

The storm outside rumbled like it agreed with us.

"Then what can I say?" I asked.

She smiled that bare, reckless smile again. "Say you'll stay."

For a second, I couldn't speak. Couldn't breathe. Then, all I could do was pull her closer and let myself believe this wouldn't end.

"Yeah," I said like it was a promise neither of us knew how to keep. "I'll stay."

We lay there in the quiet, skin slick and bodies tangled until my pulse stopped racing and the rain slowed. Until I forgot what it felt like to be anywhere but this old leather couch, with her breathing soft and even in my arms. Until I wasn't scared to fall asleep and wake up remembering nothing but how she fit against me.

Chapter Nine

LOLA

For a second—just one—I thought it might really be that easy.

That he'd stay, and I'd let him.

But then I woke up alone.

I don't know how long I lay there, staring at the ceiling and telling myself this was what I wanted. That Tanner had done precisely what I needed him to do—give me a night where nothing existed but us. No rules. No pasts. No promises we couldn't keep. Maybe I'd been stupid enough to hope for more, but even I wasn't reckless enough to admit it out loud.

I pulled on my clothes and padded barefoot across the studio in the dim morning light, trying not to notice how empty it felt—how empty I felt.

Somewhere in the universe, irony was laughing its ass off at me. Tanner was on his way out of Briar Hill before dawn, before anything could catch up with him, tie him down, or make him feel like he should stay. And God help me, I understood. I understood precisely why he left—and why I wanted him to return anyway.

I put on coffee and tried to snap myself out of it. Heat, caffeine, and a shower hot enough to scald—minimum requirements for convincing myself I didn't care. That this was fine. That Tanner hadn't snuck under my skin so fast that I didn't even feel the ink dry before he ghosted.

More irony: I trusted him enough to think he'd actually stick.

The coffee sat cold in my mug, untouched.

"Don't be stupid," I muttered again, but it sounded more desperate than defiant.

I was still staring into it, trying to remember how people functioned after having their breath knocked out when my phone rang. Veronica.

I should've let it go to voicemail. I didn't.

"Hello?"

"You sound like shit."

"Good morning to you, too, Vee. Everything okay?"

"You tell me," she said. "Pretty sure I heard your heart breaking across town."

I sighed, leaning back against the counter. "Barely after eight, and you're already a pain in my ass?"

"Gifted, aren't I? So will you tell me what happened, or will I have to call in the reinforcements?"

"It was nothing," I said, trying to sound like it was true.

Her tone shifted, curiosity edged with concern. "You sound weird, Lo."

"I'm fine," I said, forcing my voice into something less brittle. More me. "Just tired."

"You're lying to me," she said, but her voice gentled slightly. "Is it bad?"

"It was amazing," I said finally, owning it. "And over."

She paused. Like that was a twist she hadn't seen coming.

"You serious?"

"He left before sunrise."

She cursed under her breath. Not at me—at him. Then she shifted gears so fast I had to catch up. "How do you feel about a burlesque brunch?"

I blinked. "What?"

"Vivian's got a noon matinee today," she said, tone brisk and unapologetic. "Mimosas, lingerie, and family therapy by way of interpretive dance."

"I don't think—"

"Exactly," Veronica cut in. "You're not thinking. You're wallowing. Be there by eleven."

Then she hung up.

God help me, she was right.

I hung up and turned around.

And there he was.

Tanner. Standing in the doorway with a tray of coffee and donuts, hair damp and shirt sticking where the rain caught him. His eyes met mine with that familiar intensity—cautious, careful like he didn't know if I'd let him stay.

I stared at him, heart pounding too loud in my ears to hear anything else.

"You left," I said, barely a whisper.

"I didn't." He held up the coffee, sheepish. "Just went to get breakfast."

"But you—"

"I left a note," he said. "Didn't you see it?"

The breath rushed out of me in one shaky exhale. I hadn't seen it. Just like I hadn't seen this coming—him standing here looking like he meant it when he said, "I'll stay." He took a step closer, then stopped. "Am I pushing too hard, Lola? Because I can back off."

I shook my head, still trying to catch up with everything crashing through me. Relief. Confusion. Hope.

"No," I said finally. "You're not."

Something shifted in his eyes—the same thing that almost killed me yesterday when he'd looked at me like I was all the answers he didn't know he wanted. I crossed the room, closing the distance between us before I could think myself out of it. Then I was kissing him. Kissing him like he hadn't just scared the hell out of me. Like I needed him more than air.

He put the tray down without breaking the kiss and pulled me in with that warm, solid hold that made everything else disappear. It shouldn't have been possible, but it felt even better than yesterday—like waking up to an impossible gift. Like finding out what you didn't dare hope for came true.

He drew back just enough to see my face, then brushed a thumb softly over my cheekbone. "You thought I left."

"Didn't you?" I asked, voice smaller than I wanted it to be.

"No," he said again, firm and honest. "I'm here."

And this time, I let myself believe it.

TANNER

I didn't know if she'd let me back in—didn't know if I'd blown it by leaving her asleep on that old leather couch. But hell, I had to try. The look on her face when she found me standing in the doorway almost gutted me. A mix of shock and relief and something I thought might be hope. Like she hadn't expected to get anything more than a storm, a night, and maybe a little too much honesty to go with it.

I pulled her closer, kissing her with everything I didn't have words for. Everything I couldn't say without feeling like it might get caught sideways in my throat. "I'm here," I said again so she'd know how much I meant it.

I kissed her again, lifting her up and feeling the warmth of her body wrap around me.

She moved with me, easy as breath. Her back hit the wall, and she didn't flinch. She just smiled that reckless smile and pulled me closer, as if this was precisely where she wanted to be. Like I was exactly who she wanted.

"I want you so fucking much," she said against my mouth. It was enough to make me forget why I'd even left. Her legs tightened around my waist, and the heat between us burned away everything else.

I swallowed her moan in another kiss and pushed against her like I needed to get under her skin as much as she'd gotten under mine. Like I'd never get close enough.

Her fingers tangled in my hair. The edge of her teeth caught my lip.

"Lola," I growled, rough and raw.

"Tanner," she said, breathless and demanding. I met her eyes, dark and full of need. "Now," she whispered.

It was a command. It was a plea.

I let her down just long enough for the clothes to disappear between us. Pants, lace, jeans—gone.

She was back in my arms before I could draw another breath. Before I could think about anything but how much I wanted this—wanted her. I rolled a condom into place, feeling reckless and alive.

"Jesus," I said, pushing into her in one hard thrust that almost undid me right there. She held on tight, arching against me, and it was chaos all over again. My whole world narrowed down to the heat of her body and the way she wrapped around me like she'd never let go. Like we'd never have to stop.

Her moans were breathy, desperate things that matched my own. "Tanner," she said again, voice wild with need. Knowing exactly what she wanted, I didn't slow down or hold back. Exactly what I needed to give her. Every thrust was a promise, a confession, a reckless declaration. She started coming before I did, her cries muffled against my neck as she shuddered and clenched around me until I couldn't hold back another second. "Fuck," I groaned as everything hit me at once, perfect and obliterating. We stayed like that, holding on to each other like the rest of the world might pull us apart if we did anything else.

I didn't know how I'd gotten here or how long this would last. All I knew was that for the first time since that day in the desert, I didn't feel like I was running from ghosts or letting them catch up with me.

I felt free.

And the way she smiled at me—the full, unguarded thing—made me think maybe she felt the same way.

"I could get used to this," she said softly.

"Yeah?"

"Yeah."

Her eyes were dark and wild and maybe even hopeful.

And for once, mine probably were too.

Epilogue

LOLA

We never did make it to the Velvet Room that day.

Vivian forgave us, eventually.

She made us sweat a little at first—dramatic sighs, long-suffering eye rolls, a "you owe me" tab so long it might outlive us all—but she forgave us.

And now here we were, almost a year later, still standing. Still us.

Still messy, still complicated, still... more.

I tugged at the hem of my black dress, feeling absurdly overdressed and underprepared as I stared at the gallery's clean, white walls.

Sketches—*my sketches*—were framed and spotlighted like they belonged here. Like *I* belonged here.

A low whistle sounded behind me, and Tanner's hand landed warm and steady at my waist. "You're staring at your art like it's gonna bite you," he murmured against my ear.

"It might," I said, still half in disbelief. "It's just waiting for the right moment."

He chuckled—low and rough and completely unbothered, like always—and pulled me back against his chest.

"You're amazing," he said simply, and it hit harder than any compliment I'd ever been given.

I leaned into him for a second, breathing him in—leather, soap, and something uniquely Tanner—and let myself have the moment.

When I finally pulled back, his hand stayed at my waist, grounding me.

"You know," I said lightly, "this is your fault."

"My fault?"

I tipped my head back to look at him. "You're the one who said maybe I should do something with all those 'doodles' I kept hiding in sketchbooks."

He smiled, and it did dangerous things to my pulse. "Didn't think you'd actually listen."

"Neither did I."

But here we were. Not hiding. Not pretending.

I caught movement from the corner of my eye and turned to see Veronica sweeping into the gallery, looking like she owned the place. Vivian followed a half-step behind, all red lipstick and champagne flair, and Eliza—sweet, steady Eliza—was carrying a giant bouquet that looked like it weighed more than she did.

Tanner chuckled low in his throat. "Incoming."

"Brace for impact," I said, but I couldn't stop smiling.

Veronica was the first to reach us, all smug satisfaction. "Well, well, well. Look who finally decided to believe she's brilliant."

Vivian leaned in, kissing my cheek like I was some kind of conquering hero. "Told you."

Eliza thrust the flowers at me with a bright, beaming smile. "We're so proud of you!"

I stared at them, at all of them—this messy, beautiful family of mine—and felt something shift in my chest. Something *settle*.

Tanner's hand tightened at my waist like he felt it too.

"Speech!" Vivian declared, and Veronica immediately seconded her with an alarming level of enthusiasm.

I shook my head, laughing. "Not a chance."

"Come on," Tanner murmured, teasing. "I'll hold your hand."

He meant it.

And suddenly, standing there with his warm hand in mine and my sisters beaming at me like I'd just pulled off the impossible, I realized something:

Maybe I hadn't been surviving all this time after all. Maybe I'd been building something. Something real. Something that lasted.

I looped my arm through Tanner's, faced the crowd—tiny but fierce—and said, "Thank you."

Simple. True. Enough.

"You're incredible, Lola," he said, voice low and rough with certainty. "I hope you know that."

I swallowed hard, my fingers twisting in the hem of my dress. "I'm starting to."

He leaned in and brushed his mouth over mine in a kiss so soft it felt like a secret.

Someone wolf-whistled behind us—probably Veronica—and Tanner laughed against my lips.

"I'm proud of you," he murmured. "And not just because you're brilliant with ink and paper."

"Yeah?" I whispered.

"Yeah," he said, pulling back just enough so I could see the truth in his eyes. "Because you didn't just show your art tonight. You showed yourself. And you didn't hide."

I blinked hard against the sting at the back of my eyes. "Only because you were stubborn enough to call me out on it."

His smile was slow and sure. "Worth it."

We stood there for a minute—just breathing, just *being*.

And when Tanner dipped his head low and whispered, "You're not getting rid of me now, you know," I smiled so wide my cheeks hurt.

"Good," I whispered back. "Because I keep what's mine."

***

Dear Reader,

Thank you so much for picking up *Ink &* *Iron*—and for falling for Lola and Tanner right along with me.

This story began with a scar, but at its heart, it's about healing, honesty, and finding connection in the most unexpected places. Lola's sharp edges and Tanner's quiet strength made them one of my favorite pairs to write, and I hope their journey left a mark in the best possible way.

If you laughed, swooned, or maybe got a little teary-eyed along the way, I'd be so grateful if you left a review. It's the best way to help other readers find this story—and it means the world. You can review the book on Amazon.

The Thorne sisters aren't done just yet. Each one has her own brand of chaos, charm, and complicated love story waiting in the wings. So if you enjoyed your time in Briar Hill, stay close—there's more to come.

With all my love (and ink-stained fingers),

Hana York

***

Silk & Silence

A Steamy, Slow-Burn Small-Town Romance About Walls, Wreckage, and the Kind of Love That Finds You When You Stop Hiding

Hana York

Pink Pop Publishing

Silk & Silence

(The Thorne Sisters Book 2)

Copyright © 2025 by Hana York

www.HanaYork.com

Contents

Prologue

VIVIAN

The mirror never lied.

But it was damn good at keeping secrets.

I leaned closer, smoothing a hand over the sequins clinging to my hips, nudging a stray strand of hair back into place. Stage lights didn't forgive. They amplified. Every crack, every flaw, every weakness. And I'd learned how to hide them all.

The Velvet Room was my domain—red velvet, old jazz, and just enough glitter to blur the sharp edges. Classy. Controlled. Untouchable.

Just like I had to be.

Because the second you let someone see the cracks, they started looking for the exit.

I knew that better than anyone.

Pretty was protection.

Youth was survival.

Love? Love was a liability.

I capped the lipstick with a click, sealing the final layer into place.

The color was perfect.

The smile, even better.

No one in the audience would see anything but the woman I built from scratch—the woman who didn't need anyone.

And if, sometimes, my chest tightened a little too sharply?

If I caught myself wondering what it might feel like to be wanted for more than a flawless curve or a polished smile?

Well. Some things you just learned to live with.

A knock came at the dressing room door.

Showtime.

I stood, ran my hands down the sequined fabric one last time, and became the woman the world couldn't break.

The real Vivian Thorne?

She stayed locked away.

Safe.

Untouched.

And very, very alone.

Chapter One

DEAN

I hated days like this.

Days when professionalism took a back seat to spectacle.

"Come to the Velvet Room," my client had said as if it was the most reasonable request in the world. Middle of the afternoon on a workday. Meet me at a damn burlesque club.

Christ.

I'd argued. Suggested neutral ground. A restaurant. A coffee shop. Hell, the courthouse steps would've been preferable. But he insisted. Apparently, he felt "more comfortable" there.

Which, considering how his marriage was ending, said a hell of a lot more than he realized.

I shoved open the door, bracing myself for... hell, I didn't even know. Neon lights. Pulsing music.

Something I'd have to mentally scrub off afterward.

Instead, I got elegance: dark wood floors, vintage tables, and velvet curtains. It didn't smell like cheap beer or sweat. It smelled like old whiskey, expensive perfume, and something else, something rich and deliberate.

I frowned. Suspicious.

Places like this didn't exist without a catch.

I spotted my client, Charlie, waving like he hadn't just detonated the last scrap of my dignity. But before I could force myself forward, something caught at the edge of my vision. Movement from the stage.

And then I saw her.

A woman mid-performance—moving like a goddamn force of nature.

Tall. Poised. She was draped in sapphire sequins that caught the light with every sway of her hips.

But it wasn't the outfit. It wasn't even the body.

It was the *command.*

She wasn't playing to the crowd. She owned the room like she didn't need anyone's approval.

I wasn't prepared for her. Not her presence. Not her power. She moved across that stage like she owned the world, and for one breathless second, everything else fell away. The case. The client. The noise in my head.

Gone.

Only her.

And I was absolutely, without a doubt, screwed.

I tore my gaze away and stalked toward my client, jaw tight.

Focus.

Handle the meeting. Get the papers signed and get out.

That was the plan.

But it was hard to remember what the hell I was supposed to be doing when her laughter—a low, smoky sound—cut through the air and wrapped itself around my chest like barbed wire.

I dropped into the chair beside Charlie, forcing myself into something resembling professionalism.

"We had to meet here?" I muttered under my breath, scanning the room.

Charlie—already two drinks in, judging by the flush on his cheeks—grinned and waved toward the stage. "Relax,

Thatcher. I know it's not your usual vibe, but some of us need a little glitter to get through divorce proceedings."

I pulled the paperwork out of my briefcase and set it between us.

"Sign here. Initial there."

He barely glanced at it—still craning his neck toward the stage.

"You should stick around. Loosen up. Might do you good."

Against my better judgment, my gaze drifted back toward the stage—and caught another glimpse of dark hair, bare shoulders, and a smile that could wreck a man without even trying.

No.

Absolutely not.

"I'm billing you for the full hour either way," I said flatly.

He just laughed and clapped me on the back, completely unfazed.

And me?

I was already planning my escape.

Before, I did something *really* foolish.

Like ask for her name.

Charlie signed with a careless flick of his pen and shoved the folder back toward me.

"That's Vivian," he said, nodding toward the stage. "She runs the place."

I followed his gaze.

"She usually comes out to say hi after her set," Charlie added. "You should stick around. I'll introduce you."

I tapped the folder against the table. Pretended like I wasn't intrigued.

Yes, I wanted to meet her.

No, I absolutely should not.

Because something about her pressed against every boundary I'd built.

And I didn't know what scared me more, the idea of losing control or the realization that maybe I wanted to.

VIVIAN

The last notes of the music faded, the red velvet curtains sweeping back into place behind me.

Another afternoon, another show.

The crowd had been good—lively but respectful. A little loud during the feather fan tease, but that was to be expected.

I grabbed my robe from the backstage hook, shrugging it on as I moved toward the wings.

Viv," Claire called, slipping through the back hall to meet me. "Charlie's hoping you'll stop by and say hi. He's got some Suit with him."

I tugged the robe tighter around my waist and moved toward my dressing room.

A Suit.

I already knew who she meant.

I'd spotted him halfway through my set—new, out of place, impossible to miss.

Dark hair. A jawline you could cut glass on. Shoulders that deserved better than a suit and a starched button-down.

The kind of man who probably said things like *irrevocable trust* for a living.

Most of our patrons relaxed once the lights dimmed—jackets unbuttoned, posture uncoiled, the day's sharp edges dulling into something easier to carry.

Not him.

He sat straight-backed and still.

Not leering.

Not dazzled.

Just... watching.

And if I'd been smart, I would've left it at that.

Noted. Filed away. Forgotten.

But something in the way he watched—calm, unshaken, like he wasn't impressed or intimidated—made him more dangerous than the ones who couldn't stop staring.

The obvious ones? Easy to predict. Easy to ignore.

Men like him?

Men like him were dangerous.

I changed out of my costume. Nothing dramatic—just traded the tease for tailored power.

Slacks that hugged just right. A plunging blouse I wore like a dare.

Charlie spotted me first, waving from one of the corner tables. I smiled for him—polished, easy—and crossed the room like I wasn't bracing for impact.

And then I saw him up close.

God help me.

Crisp lines. Focused stillness. The kind of presence that didn't demand attention—it simply expected it.

When I approached, he stood—*stood*—like we were at some country club luncheon, and he was about to pull out my chair. Polite. Sharp. Unshakable.

Very, very dangerous.

"Vivian," Charlie said, all charm and good intentions. "I wanted to introduce you to a friend of mine. Dean Thatcher."

Dean.

I smiled, cool and easy, and extended my hand.

"Vivian Thorne."

His hand closed around mine. His handshake was firm. Measured. Like everything else about him. No squeeze. No flex. No unnecessary performance.

And for just a moment—just a blink—I saw something in his eyes.

Not lust.

Not conquest.

Recognition.

Like he saw past the performance and the stage lights straight to the woman still standing there.

He released my hand slowly, offering a small, polite smile.

"Nice to meet you." The words were even, careful—like he was trying not to reveal too much.

And God help me again because all I could think was: This man could ruin me without ever laying a hand on me.

Charlie said something—probably trying to fill the air between us—but I barely caught it.

Something about business. About Dean being a lawyer. About how he was just visiting.

Visiting.

Good.

Maybe he'd leave before I did something unwise.

Like, wonder how that voice would sound without all the restraint—just him, unguarded. Then I tucked a curl behind my ear and smiled like he hadn't just turned the ground beneath my stilettos to quicksand.

"Welcome to the Velvet Room," I said, pitching my voice low and smooth. "Hope the show wasn't too scandalous for you."

"Hardly," he said. "More... unexpected."

Something in the way he said it, quiet and sincere, slipped past my defenses before I could stop it, knocking something loose inside me.

I tilted my head, studying him like I would a painting I wasn't sure I understood.

"Life's more fun when it's a little unexpected," I said lightly, even though my pulse was hammering loud enough to drown out the music.

Claire appeared at my elbow with a fresh drink for Charlie.

I took the cue.

One last glance at the man across from me—quiet, sharp, unreadable—and I turned away.

But as I moved through the room, something in me stayed behind.

And that was the part that worried me.

Chapter Two

DEAN

I should've walked away the second I shook her hand.

A polite nod. A thank-you-for-your-time. A quick, professional exit.

That's what I should have done.

Instead, I stood there like an idiot while the world shrank to the woman before me.

Vivian Thorne.

Owner of the Velvet Room. Star of the show.

And absolutely the last woman I had any business looking at like that.

She was... luminous.

Not flashy. Not cheap.

Just vibrant.

She smiled at me—smooth, practiced—and I knew it wasn't real.

Not entirely.

But there was something under it. Something real enough to make my chest ache.

"Life's more fun when it's a little unexpected," she'd said.

Christ.

I told myself it was just adrenaline. Just the absurdity of the situation—meeting a client in a damn burlesque club, surrounded by velvet and music, and a woman who made every part of me feel ten years younger and twice as stupid.

I knew it wasn't just curiosity. Whatever this was—whatever had just passed between us—was the kind of thing I'd spent years avoiding. And yet, as she turned away without a word, disappearing into the room like smoke through a keyhole, I sat there, restless—like something had started that I wasn't ready to let end.

Charlie clapped a hand on my shoulder. "She's something, huh?"

I didn't answer.

Because *something* didn't even begin to cover it.

***

I stared at the case file on my desk, willing it to offer some justification—any thread I could pull to make this about work.

It didn't.

Charlie's divorce was clean. No contested assets. No custody fight. Just paperwork and deadlines.

Nothing in the file required a conversation with Vivian Thorne.

And yet—

His habits were relevant. Character mattered.

Professional due diligence.

That was the story I told myself.

But the truth was more straightforward. I just wanted to see her again.

I wasn't a fool. I knew what I was doing.

It wasn't about the case.

It was the way something in me tightened when she smiled.

The way my chest locked up when she walked away.

Every reasonable instinct said to leave it alone.

But my hand was already reaching for the phone.

I could keep it professional.

A few questions. A polite follow-up. Just enough to justify the call.

The line rang once. Twice. Three times.

By the fourth, I almost hung up.

And then her voice slid through the speaker—smooth, amused, unhurried. *"The Velvet Room, this is Vivian."*

I automatically sat up straighter, even though she couldn't see me.

"Ms. Thorne, this is Dean Thatcher. We met briefly yesterday through Charlie..." God, I sounded stiff. I forced myself to breathe. "I'd like to schedule a meeting. To discuss a few matters relevant to his case."

"Relevant to his case," she repeated, voice edged with something I couldn't quite name.

"Yes," I said, keeping my voice even. "At my office. Tomorrow afternoon, if you're available."

I gripped the phone tighter, half-waiting for her to laugh. To call me on the lie we were both pretending not to see.

Instead, she said, "Text me the time and address," and gave me her number.

Professional. Efficient. Unbothered.

The exact opposite of how I felt the second the call ended.

I stared at the phone for a full minute, half expecting it to call me an idiot.

Seeing her again was a mistake.

Wanting her, that was reckless.

But I didn't call off the meeting.

Instead, I opened my calendar—and locked the damn thing in.

VIVIAN

The second I ended the call, I just stood there.

Phone still in my hand. Heart doing something stupid and fluttery behind my ribs.

The memory of how he'd looked at me—like I wasn't a fantasy on a stage but something more— had my pulse tapping out a different story—one where a man actually looked *past* the red lips and stage lights.

I wasn't the type to get flustered.

Not by men.

Not anymore.

And yet—

I stared at the phone like it had personally betrayed me.

"Get it together," I muttered under my breath.

Still feeling too jumpy, I did what any sensible woman would do: I called Veronica. My twin was the only person who could usually read me without translation.

She picked up on the second ring.

"What's wrong?"

"Why do you assume something's wrong?"

"Because you don't call in the middle of the day unless you're spiraling or plotting revenge. Which is it?"

I flopped into the nearest chair, pressing the heel of my hand to my forehead.

"I just got summoned to a lawyer's office."

"What did you do now?" she said, sharp and suspicious. Typical Veronica.

I rolled my eyes. "Why do you always assume I'm at fault?"

"Because you usually are."

"Rude," I muttered.

"Accurate," she said, not even pretending otherwise.

I sighed dramatically. "Knew I should've called one of the other sisters."

Veronica laughed. "Oh please. Lola would tell you to punch him, and Eliza would bake him cupcakes."

I dragged a hand through my hair. "It's not like that. I'm not being sued, indicted, or otherwise scandalized."

"Then why the summons, Viv?"

"I'm just answering a few questions," I said, aiming for breezy and landing somewhere closer to *suspiciously defensive*. "Charlie's lawyer wants some context about the club."

Veronica didn't answer right away. When she did, her voice was sharp as a scalpel. "What aren't you telling me?"

I picked at a loose thread on my sleeve. "Nothing."

"Viv." The twin-voice. The one you didn't lie to without consequences.

I sighed. "Fine. Maybe he's...a little hot."

A scandalized gasp. "Vivian Thorne, are you actually admitting attraction? Someone alert the media!"

I rolled my eyes so hard it hurt. "I didn't admit anything."

"Oh, please. You're practically fanning yourself through the phone."

"I am not."

"You are. And you're *smiling*. You never smile after a summons unless it involves petty revenge."

I groaned. "It's professional, Veronica."

Veronica's voice turned downright gleeful. "Oh, you're doomed. Completely and utterly doomed."

"God, I hate you," I grumbled.

"You love me. I'm the only one who tells you the truth."

I muttered something colorful under my breath.

"Call me after," she said. "And don't agree to anything shady without a witness."

"Love you too, Mom," I teased, ending the call.

But the second the line went dead, the calm I'd faked started to fray.

I stood, straightened my spine, and exhaled.

Tomorrow, I'd walk into that office like I owned the damn building—sharp, calm, and unshakable.

***

The dress said control.

The heels said don't underestimate me.

The lipstick said I dare you to look away.

None of it was subtle.

That was the point.

If I was going to pretend this was business, I was damn well going to do it looking like a woman no man could rattle—even if one already had.

I pushed through the heavy glass door, every click of my heels on the polished floor a reminder: Control the room before it controls you.

The receptionist glanced up, her polite smile flickering at the sight of me. I didn't blame her. Their typical clientele probably didn't show up in tailored red dresses and stilettos sharp enough to draw blood.

"Vivian Thorne," I said smoothly. "I have an appointment with Dean Thatcher."

Her fingers fluttered over the keyboard. "He's expecting you. Last door on the left."

I smiled—sharp, polished—and headed down the hall.

One breath.

Two.

Then I stepped into Dean's office like I hadn't already lost sleep over a man I'd barely even touched.

Chapter Three

DEAN

Halfway through reviewing Charlie's financial disclosures, I heard the click of heels in the hallway.

Sharp. Even. Unhurried.

I told myself it wasn't her.

But the lie didn't hold long.

When she stepped into the doorway, my focus scattered.

Vivian Thorne.

She didn't just enter the room—she took possession of it.

Back straight. Chin high. Every detail deliberate.

A woman who understood precisely what kind of attention she could command and never once apologized for it.

I stood automatically because there was no universe where you stayed seated when she was in the room.

"Ms. Thorne," I said, my voice steadier than I felt. "Thank you for coming."

She smiled—slow, lethal, a warning wrapped in satin.

"Pleasure's mine, Counselor." The words purred from her lips.

It hit harder than it should've.

Pleasure.

One word.

That's all it took.

The sound of it curled around my ribs, dragged heat low in my gut—steady, sure, inevitable.

I shouldn't have been thinking about her mouth. How it would feel against mine. Or how those lips could shape other words—lower, rougher, against my skin.

I forced my hands still against the desk. Clenched my jaw so hard it hurt. Tethered myself to the fact that this was a meeting.

Not a surrender.

Because if I let myself feel it—really feel it—I knew I wouldn't stop.

One word, one look, and I was already losing ground.

And the worst part? I wasn't sure I wanted it back.

I motioned to the chair across from my desk. "Please. Have a seat."

She arched one perfect brow—wry, unreadable—but sat and crossed her legs with deliberate ease. The slit of her dress eased open just enough to expose a stretch of thigh that short-circuited every rational thought I had.

I looked away too fast reaching for a file like it might anchor me to something solid. Paper. Ink. Facts. Anything that wasn't her.

"You've known Mr. Halpern for...?" I asked, grateful my voice stayed steady.

Vivian folded her hands lightly in her lap, entirely composed. "A few years. He's a regular."

"At your club," I said, eyes dropping to the notes again.

"No, the knitting circle. Yes, the club."

Deadpan. Dry. A flicker of humor that almost made me smile.

I nodded, forcing myself to stay on task. "Has he ever brought a companion? A date?"

"Once or twice," she said. "Mostly, he comes alone. Orders the same drink. Tips in fives. Predictable, if nothing else."

I scribbled that down. "Any history of temper?"

"Not once."

"Inappropriate? Disrespectful?"

Her lips quirked. "He once complained the velvet upholstery made his pants too warm."

I glanced up despite myself. "That's not quite what I meant."

She smiled a glint of mischief in her eyes. "That's all you're getting."

"Any concerns you'd want on record?"

Vivian tilted her head, amused. "Are we still talking about Charlie?"

My jaw ticked. "Trying to."

Her smile faded into something more careful. Softer.

"Why does it matter what I think?" she asked quietly. "You already know what you're going to say in court."

I paused.

Because she wasn't wrong. But the way she said it made something tighten low in my gut.

"I like having all the pieces before I build my argument," I said. "I don't assume."

She held my gaze. Steady. Unflinching.

"That's rare," she said.

The words shouldn't have landed the way they did. But they did.

I leaned back slightly, suddenly aware of my tight grip on the file.

"Anything else I should know about Mr. Halpern?" I asked, my voice more ragged than I liked.

Vivian studied me—really studied me—before speaking.

"Only that he seems...lonely," she said softly. "Not like he's chasing anything. Just... like someone who's gotten used to being alone—even when it's not what they want."

The words slid under my skin.

"You ever think some people choose it?" I asked, surprising myself. "Loneliness. Because it hurts less than the alternative."

"Yeah." She didn't smile. Didn't flinch. "I think about that more than I should."

I cleared my throat. Snapped the file shut like it would snap my control back into place.

Newsflash: It didn't.

"Thank you for your time," I said, even though I hadn't asked half the questions I meant to.

Vivian stood, graceful and lethal, like she knew I'd still feel the impact long after she was gone.

I stood too—reflex, instinct—and rounded the desk to walk her to the door.

Professional.

Or so I told myself.

We walked side by side—a few feet, no more—but the air between us felt thick enough to drown in.

Her perfume—rich, clean, something I couldn't name—wrapped around me.

She passed close—her dress brushing my leg in a whisper of fabric.

My hand lifted without thinking, fingers pausing just shy of her back.

I stopped myself.

Barely.

I didn't touch her.

But God, I wanted to.

I ushered her out the door instead, muscles tight with restraint.

She glanced back at me, a slow, knowing smile curving her mouth. "Try not to overthink it, Counselor."

And then she was gone.

Leaving me standing there, wondering if she'd meant the case—or something else.

VIVIAN

I made it to the sidewalk before I exhaled.

One foot in front of the other, heels clicking like punctuation in a sentence I wasn't sure how to finish.

What the hell was that?

He hadn't touched me. Hadn't flirted. Hadn't done anything remotely inappropriate.

And still—he'd gotten under my skin more than I cared to admit.

Dean Thatcher was polite. Measured. All that controlled energy behind crisp shirts and sharp lines and a voice that should've come with a warning label. And when he looked at me—really looked—I didn't feel like a performer or a businesswoman or a fantasy in silk and sequins.

I felt seen.

Which was so much worse.

The moment I crossed the street, I yanked my phone from my purse and texted Veronica:

Vivian: *You were right.*

Veronica: *Obviously. About what?*

Vivian: *He's dangerous.*

Veronica: *Did he try anything?*

Vivian: *No. That's the problem. He didn't have to.*

I shoved my phone away before she could reply and turned the corner toward the Velvet Room. Familiar ground. My world. My rules.

Dean Thatcher was sharp and steady and utterly inconvenient.

And if I had any sense left in my head, I'd forget how his eyes lingered like he wanted to memorize me.

***

I returned to the Velvet Room just as Claire was restocking the bar for the evening show.

She glanced over. "You live."

"Don't sound so surprised."

She smirked. "Did the lawyer breathe fire or smolder quietly while trying not to stare at your legs?"

I slid onto one of the high stools. "Bit of both."

Claire raised a brow, poured sparkling water into a crystal glass, and slid it toward me. "You gonna tell me what that was about?"

"Charlie's divorce." I sipped. "Apparently, I'm a character witness now."

Claire folded a bar towel in half. "And?"

"And nothing. It was professional."

Claire tilted her head. "Then why the frown? Wasn't he just another Suit?"

I shook my head, the words scraping out before I could stop them. "That's the problem. He didn't feel like just another anything."

I stared into my glass for a second. Gathering my thoughts felt like herding cats.

"He wasn't what I expected," I said finally. "He looked at me like he couldn't decide if I was dangerous... or damaged."

"And which are you?" she asked.

I smiled without humor. "Depends on the man."

She let the silence stretch, giving me room to say more—or lie.

"You're not used to attention like that," she said after a beat.

I huffed a quiet laugh. "I'm used to all kinds of attention. Just not the kind that feels like it might stick."

Claire said nothing. Just kept polishing.

I set my drink down harder than necessary. "I've seen men like him. Polished. Controlled. They pick women who look good on their arm—and trade them in when the next shiny thing comes along."

Claire looked up, her gaze steady. "You really believe that?"

I shrugged, mouth tight. "I watched my father leave my mother for someone half her age. I watched my mother pretend it didn't hollow her out."

Claire's voice softened. "Maybe not every man is your father."

"Maybe," I said, picking up my glass again. "But I'm not interested in finding out the hard way."

Claire didn't argue. Just raised a brow and slipped away, sensing I'd said as much as I was going to.

I stayed where I was, drink in hand, trying not to replay the look in Dean Thatcher's eyes.

Then I glanced at my phone. My thumb hovered over Lola's name.

I'd already called Veronica.

Which meant I was either spiraling—or certifiably insane—because now I was calling Lola.

Not that she wasn't capable—she was. But I didn't usually do vulnerable.

Especially not with the sister whose version of emotional support involved tequila or tattoos or both.

Still, I hit dial.

She picked up on the second ring. "Viv? Everything okay?"

"Are you busy?"

Lola laughed faintly after a pause. "Well, Tanner's trying to cook. So technically, yes, but only because I might need to extinguish a fire."

I hesitated. Then, against my better judgment, I asked, "Do you think men can be trusted?"

Lola made a sound somewhere between a laugh and a wince. "Heavy question for a Tuesday, Viv."

I grimaced. "Forget I asked."

God, what was I doing? I didn't ask questions like that.

"No, wait—" she cut in, voice softer now. "Didn't expect that one from you, that's all."

I huffed out a breath. "Yeah, well. Desperate times and all that jazz."

She didn't answer right away.

Then, "I didn't used to think they could be trusted. Not after everything. Not really."

I stayed silent, pressing my thumb harder against the glass.

"Then Tanner showed up and didn't treat me like I was broken. He saw the whole damn mess—and didn't flinch."

I closed my eyes against the ache creeping up my chest. "You think that's common?"

"No," Lola said. "That's what makes it worth it."

I exhaled slowly, the knot tightening anyway. "I just... I met someone who didn't flinch. Who didn't leer, push, or try to pretend I was something I'm not. And I don't know if that makes him honest—or dangerous."

Lola didn't answer right away, but when she did, her voice was low but certain. "Sometimes it's both. And sometimes... that's what makes it real."

I sat there, my phone warm against my ear, my heart heavier than it should've been.

"Yeah," I said softly. "That's what I'm afraid of."

Chapter Four

DEAN

I'd made it exactly thirty-six hours.

Thirty-six hours of telling myself she was a distraction.

That I had a job to do. A carefully balanced life. And no business chasing a woman who made my pulse forget how to behave.

I buried myself in motions, filings, case law—anything to keep my hands busy and my mind off the way her voice had wrapped around the word *pleasure* like a velvet noose.

It didn't work.

By noon, I was supposed to be drafting a motion for continuance.

Instead, I sat at my desk, staring at the same paragraph for ten minutes and thinking about a woman I had no business wanting.

By two, I gave up pretending.

It wasn't about Charlie. It wasn't about the case.

But I'd already made peace with the lie I would tell.

I just needed to see her again.

Professional inquiry. Follow-up questions.

That was the story I'd stick to.

I picked up the phone.

Her voice slid through the line—low, smooth, dangerous.

"Vivian Thorne."

My hand clenched around the receiver like it might keep me steady.

"Ms. Thorne. Dean Thatcher. I—uh—had a few follow-up questions regarding Charlie's case."

"Oh really?" she asked, amusement coloring every syllable.

Professional, I reminded myself. *Keep it professional.*

"I was wondering if you might be willing to meet again. Somewhere a little less... formal."

I could practically hear her smirk.

"Less formal?" she said lightly. "Counselor, are you asking me on a date?"

My brain short-circuited for a second.

"No," I said too quickly. Then, forcing my voice into something vaguely calm, "Of course not. Strictly business."

"Mmm," she said, not even pretending to believe it.

"There's a diner a few blocks from my office," I added, clearing my throat. "Billy's. Neutral ground. Public place."

"Neutral ground," she echoed, laughing low—a sound that wasn't helping my cause *at all*.

"Is that lawyer-speak for 'I'm afraid you'll eat me alive'?"

"No, I— That's not what—"

"Relax, Counselor," she teased. "I'll behave. Probably."

Probably.

I ran a hand down my face.

"Three o'clock?" I asked, barely recognizing my own voice.

"I'll be there," she promised.

And then she hung up—leaving me staring at the phone like a man who had just volunteered for execution and couldn't wait for it.

***

I stepped inside Billy's Diner, and the kid behind the counter looked at me as if I'd wandered into the wrong movie set.

And maybe I had.

I headed for a booth in the back, sitting stiffly, the leather squeaking under me.

It wasn't until I settled in that I realized how out of place I looked.

Crisp suit. Perfect knot. The exact right amount of starch in my collar.

Dressing like this was automatic. A reflex. A habit.

But sitting there, under the buzz of neon lights and the smell of burnt coffee, it hit me:

The suit wasn't for the diner. Hell, it wasn't even for Vivian. It was armor. A habit. A shield.

Something I put on every day so no one could see what was underneath. And somewhere along the line, I'd stopped noticing its weight.

Until her.

I loosened my tie just a fraction. Shrugged off my suit coat. Rolled up my sleeves like it might make me look less like a stereotype—and more like a man.

I was still convincing myself I had this under control when the door chimed, and she walked in.

Vivian Thorne didn't belong in Billy's Diner any more than I did—but she made it look deliberate. Like she decided what belonged, not the other way around.

She wore jeans and a simple black top—nothing flashy, nothing calculated.

And still, my world tilted on its axis.

She spotted me and headed over with a walk that should've been illegal—smooth, confident, more than a little dangerous.

I stood as she reached the table because manners were the only thing I still remembered how to do.

"Counselor," she said, amusement sparking in her eyes as she slid into the booth across from me.

"Vivian," I said, and if my voice was rougher than it should've been—well, there were limits to what a man could control.

"This town must be running low on meeting rooms if you're stuck holding court here."

I gave a dry smile. "I thought it might be less intimidating than summoning you back to my lair."

She laughed, low and warm, and something in my chest pulled tight.

"You'd have to work a lot harder to intimidate me, Counselor," she said, flashing a smile sharp enough to cut.

I sat down slowly, feeling every inch too polished for the setting.

She shifted, crossing one leg over the other—and her ankle brushed mine under the table.

A flash of contact. Barely there. But enough to light up every nerve ending I had.

It could've been nothing. A mistake.

But some reckless part of me wanted to believe that it wasn't.

Wanted to believe that she felt it, too.

VIVIAN

I saw it the second my ankle brushed him under the table—accidentally, *maybe*.

That flicker in his eyes.

Like control was something he clutched with both hands—and I'd just loosened his grip without even trying.

I leaned back, letting the moment stretch.

Weighing him.

Then, I decided I was done letting him call the shots.

"Alright, Counselor," I said, voice easy, words anything but. "Enough polite small talk. What's this really about?"

"I told you," he said carefully. "Context for the case."

I lifted a brow. "I call BS. You already have context. Charlie's predictable. Harmless. You didn't drag me to a diner to hear me repeat that."

He didn't argue. Didn't reach for some slick excuse. Just sat there, staring at me like he didn't know how to put it into words.

"I just..." He exhaled. "I wanted to see you again."

The way he said it sent a shiver down my spine, and something twisted low in my stomach.

I felt that old instinct rise—the one that said *don't let it get close.*

Usually, I listened. Usually, I moved first.

This time, I didn't.

Instead, I smiled. "Next time, Counselor, you can just ask."

Then—because it was safer than whatever was burning between us—I added, "But if we're doing lunch, you're buying."

Dean's mouth twitched like he wanted to smile. Instead, he reached for a laminated menu tucked behind the napkin holder.

"Anything you want," he said, voice steady.

I took the menu, pretending to study it. Giving us both a second to breathe.

But the air between us didn't lighten. It thickened.

"So," I said, flipping a page. "Tell me something, Counselor."

He lifted a brow. "Like what?"

I shrugged. "Something real. Not court-approved. Not practiced."

I could almost see the battle behind his eyes—the urge to dodge it, to keep things professional.

But then he said, almost like he didn't mean to, "I thought being a divorce attorney would be about helping people."

I blinked.

That... wasn't what I expected.

He leaned back, eyes fixed on the chipped table between us.

"Figured I'd be the calm in the storm," he said. "The one helping people find a way through the wreckage."

A humorless smile pulled at his mouth.

"Mostly, it's just stepping between two people who would rather set each other on fire than settle anything. Feels less like helping and more like trying to keep two angry rhinos from charging."

The words came out rough—quiet, almost like they surprised him.

Maybe that was what cracked something loose inside me.

Before I could stop myself, I said, "I can't stand happy endings."

His brow furrowed slightly.

I forced a laugh, low and dry. "Movies. Books. Anything tied up with a neat bow. It makes me itchy. Like I'm just waiting for the other shoe to drop."

I shook my head once. "Real life doesn't do bows. It rips the wrapping paper, forgets the card... sometimes lights the whole damn thing on fire."

The words hung between us—too raw, too honest, too much.

Dean nodded. Once. Like he understood more than he should.

The air stretched tight, humming with something dangerous.

So, I did what I always did when things got too real.

I flashed a smile and said, "Well, look at us. Two cynics getting maudlin over diner food."

Dean huffed a breath that might've been a laugh. "Terrifying."

"Terrifying, indeed," I agreed, lifting my glass in a mock toast. "Next thing you know, we'll be writing bad poetry and blaming our parents."

That earned a genuine smile from him—slow, deliberate, and far too devastating.

I told myself the moment passed.

The banter had done its job, smoothing the edges back into place.

But underneath it, the pull didn't fade. It just waited—unspoken, undeniable, inevitable.

Chapter Five

VIVIAN

I set my water glass down and leaned back, letting the tension in the air settle.

"Well," I said, letting the word stretch, playful and sharp, "for a man who claims he's a professional, you're doing a terrible job keeping this interview on track."

Dean's mouth twitched. "You're not exactly making it easy."

I tilted my head, letting my gaze drag over him. Clean lines. Coiled tension. That stubborn, careful control he wore like armor.

"Maybe you're just out of practice."

His eyes darkened, the muscle in his jaw ticking once.

God, it was so easy to get under his skin. Too easy.

Which meant it was time to go—*before* I did something reckless.

I stood, smoothing a hand over the curve of my top. His gaze dropped—quick, automatic, hungry—hitting me like a live wire. Right through the skin. Straight to the parts of me that still remembered what it felt like to be seen—and wanted.

I smiled, slow and sure. "Thanks for lunch, Counselor."

He stood too—because, of course, he did—always the gentleman, even when drowning.

I paused—briefly—close enough to smell his cologne. Something clean and devastating.

I tipped my face up, close enough for him to feel the heat of my breath.

"Maybe next time," I murmured, voice low and wicked, "you'll ask for what you really want."

I let the words hang there—heavy, electric—before turning away with a wicked little smile.

I didn't look back.

I didn't have to.

I could feel him standing there. Still burning.

DEAN

I stood there like a man who'd forgotten how to move.

Vivian Thorne walked out of that diner like she hadn't just knocked the ground out from under me with ten words and a smile.

Maybe next time you'll ask for what you really want.

Christ.

I raked a hand through my hair, forcing myself to sit back down before I did something stupid. Like chase after her. Like kiss her how I'd wanted to from the moment she smiled at me like she already knew how this ended.

I stared at the half-empty water glass she had left behind. Evidence. Proof she'd been here—and I was already losing the war I hadn't meant to start.

This wasn't how it worked. I was supposed to be in control, careful, and one step ahead.

Not this spiraling heat. Not this gut-deep certainty that if I wasn't careful, I'd rewrite every rule I lived by just to stay close to her.

I should've walked away after the first meeting. Filed the paperwork. Filed her under complications to avoid at all costs.

Instead, I was sitting there like a damn fool, still smelling her perfume and wishing I'd asked for what I really wanted.

Her.

Not as a witness. Not as a character reference. Not as another line in a case file.

Just *her*.

And maybe I wasn't ready.

But no way in hell I was going to walk away without a fight.

Chapter Six

VIVIAN

I had *not* spent the last three days thinking about Dean Thatcher.

Not about how he leaned across the table like he wanted to memorize how I breathed. Not about the way he said my name like it was something sacred. Definitely not about the way he loosened his tie—just enough to make me wonder what else might come undone if I applied the right pressure.

No, I'd been busy. Running a club. Managing rehearsals. Pretending I didn't check my phone like an idiot every time it buzzed.

Which made it all the more cruel when fate threw him straight into my path without warning.

Briar Hill's Annual Community Charity Drive. A fundraiser for the local food bank. A reminder that sometimes this town still had its heart exactly where it should be.

I was roped into it by Eliza, who weaponized her dimples and homemade cookies until I caved.

I didn't even like daytime events. There was too much sunlight and too many people pretending they didn't want to one-up each other with baked goods and raffle prizes.

I was standing there, politely pretending to listen to a woman explain her gluten-free scone strategy, when the crowd shifted—and I saw him.

Dean.

Not in a suit.

My brain went haywire for a solid five seconds.

Dark jeans. A soft gray T-shirt that clung in ways it had no business clinging. Sunglasses pushed up into his hair. One hand casually hooked into his pocket like he wasn't the most devastating thing the community center had ever seen.

And because life had a vicious sense of humor, he spotted me almost immediately.

I straightened instinctively, smoothing invisible wrinkles from my sundress, cursing the part of me that felt too seen.

His gaze dragged over me, slow and deliberate, before a half-smile curved at the corner of his mouth—like he knew exactly what he was doing.

And damn him, it worked.

I felt the pull in every nerve ending, low and insistent.

He started toward me, and something quiet unspooled in my chest.

I didn't move. Didn't let it show.

But I felt it.

Whatever this was—it wasn't innocent.

And I couldn't remember the last time I'd wanted to touch danger so badly.

And then he was there—close enough for his scent to catch me off guard. Clean. Subtle. And far too compelling.

I tipped my head back to meet his gaze and let one brow arch slowly. "Well, well. Counselor Thatcher. Look at you—tie off, jaw unclenched. I'm impressed."

"Didn't realize the tie was such a defining feature," he said, voice low and rough.

I shrugged, pretending the sound of it didn't brush right over every exposed nerve. "It was either the tie or the permanent state of mild disapproval."

He chuckled, and damn if the sound didn't punch straight through the fragile armor I'd barely managed to tape together.

"Don't worry," he said. "I can still disapprove without the tie."

I leaned in slightly, letting my voice drop into a purr. "You disapprove of me, Counselor?"

His gaze dropped—just for a second—to my mouth. When he met my eyes again, there was heat banked so deep it made me feel reckless.

"Only when I'm trying to keep my sanity," he murmured.

I smiled sweetly. "Good luck with that."

Dean's answering smile was nothing short of lethal.

Before we could say something truly regrettable, Eliza appeared, weaving through the crowd with panic written all over her sweet, wide-eyed face.

"Viv!" she gasped, clutching a clipboard to her chest like a life raft. "Thank God. I need a huge favor."

I blinked. "Eliza, what—"

"I forgot the donation baskets!" she blurted, cheeks flaming. "They're still at my apartment. I can't leave, and we need them before the auction starts—"

"I'll go," I said automatically because that's what you did for Eliza.

She nodded gratefully. "They're boxed up, but...they won't fit in your car."

I stilled. Of course they wouldn't. My two-seater wasn't exactly known for its cargo capacity.

A voice rumbled beside me before I could even open my mouth to suggest a solution.

"I've got a truck," Dean said casually. "I'll drive you."

I turned to look at him. He met my gaze without flinching. No smirk. No teasing.

"You're sure?" I asked, aiming for cool and probably missing by a mile.

He shrugged one broad shoulder. "Community spirit, right?"

Eliza beamed like a golden retriever who'd just been offered a lifetime supply of biscuits. "You're a lifesaver! Both of you!"

Dean smiled politely, but his eyes never left mine.

I got the feeling community spirit had very little to do with it.

I exhaled and nodded. "Alright, Counselor. Let's go save the day."

DEAN

The second she slid into the truck, the air changed.

Vivian Thorne, in my passenger seat, all soft perfume and sharper edges, wearing a smile that should've come with a warning label.

I gripped the wheel tighter than necessary and pulled onto the road, trying not to notice the flash of bare skin every time the truck jolted over a bump.

Trying not to imagine things I had no business imagining.

We had maybe ten minutes until we hit her sister's apartment.

Ten minutes to sit next to her and pretend my mind wasn't in a back alley brawl with my better judgment.

I stared straight ahead. Counted the seconds. Reminded myself that I was a grown man. A professional. Not some hormone-drunk teenager looking for an excuse to pull over and—

I cut that thought off with a sharp breath.

Jesus.

When was the last time anything made me feel like this? Like I wanted to pull her onto my lap and lose myself in the kind of need I didn't have words for.

"Something wrong, Counselor?" she asked, voice silky—like she already knew the answer.

I cleared my throat. "All good. Just driving."

"Uh-huh." She turned to the window, but not before I caught the smirk tugging at her mouth.

God help me, she was enjoying this. Enjoying unraveling me.

I pulled into the parking lot with a little more force than necessary, gravel crunching under the tires. I hesitated before getting out of the truck, trying to control my heated thoughts.

"You coming, Counselor?" she asked, sliding a slow glance my way—mock innocence sharpened to a blade.

I opened my door like it might save me. Spoiler alert: it didn't.

"Third-floor walk-up," she said, cocking her head. "Think you're up for it, Counselor?"

I bit back a smile. "I can handle it."

Her grin turned wicked. "We'll see." She pivoted and started up the stairs without another word.

I didn't hesitate. Just followed—because stopping? That ship had sailed.

She stepped into the apartment, and I followed close behind, the door clicking shut just as she abruptly stopped. And I walked right into her.

My hands caught her hips before I could stop them.

Just meant to steady her.

But then she turned—

Eyes wide, lips parted—

And I didn't think—I just kissed her like she was the one thing that could save me from going under.

She made a low, startled sound against my mouth—and then her hands were in my hair, on my shoulders, dragging me closer until there was no space between us.

I braced her against the wall, my hand slipping under the hem of her dress, the heat of her skin burning through every shred of control I had left.

She arched into me, breathless, reckless, and I forgot there was a world beyond this moment.

"Dean," she gasped—my name like a plea she didn't mean to speak aloud.

And between that and the kiss, I didn't stand a chance.

And God help me, I wanted all of her.

I kissed her again—deeper, rougher—because words no longer stood a chance.

Not when everything real, everything that mattered, was already right here between us.

Chapter Seven

VIVIAN

I pulled back, breathless and shaking, and Dean's eyes—God, his eyes—were dark with something that scared me to death and made me want it all at once.

"This isn't—" I started, barely recognizing my voice. "I don't usually—"

His hand stayed tangled in my hair, gentler now but no less devastating.

"Me either," he said, the heat in his tone unmistakable. "But goddamn, Vivian—I've never wanted someone as much as I want you."

And how he said my name—like he'd been waiting a lifetime to say it—made me forget why I'd ever considered stopping.

His mouth crashed into mine again, hungry and urgent.

This time, I didn't hold back. This time, I let myself feel it—all of it—the way my blood sang and how his hands anchored me like I was the only thing keeping him sane.

My back hit the wall, and Dean's hands were everywhere—my hips, my thighs, my hair—the heat of him wild and consuming. He lifted me effortlessly, and I wrapped my legs around his waist, grinding into his cock through denim and lace, desperate for more, desperate for everything.

The world blurred, its edges dissolving into heat and need. I fisted the hem of his T-shirt, tugging it up, feeling his raw strength beneath my hands—muscle and heat, too much and not enough.

His skin burned against mine as I yanked the shirt over his head, and his mouth was back on me before it even hit the floor.

I gasped when his hand slipped beneath my dress, fingers tracing the edge of my panties—teasing, testing—until I almost begged him for more.

Then he pushed the lace aside and plunged his fingers inside me—deep, sure, relentless.

A cry ripped from my throat.

I clung to him, shuddering, as he moved—slow at first, then harder, deeper, finding a rhythm that sent white-hot pleasure spearing through me.

"So wet," he growled against my neck. "So fucking wet and tight."

His voice broke, and the sound of it shot through me like a jolt. "Jesus, Vivian."

I couldn't think, couldn't speak—just held on as he fucked me with his fingers, pushing me higher with every hard, perfect thrust.

"Dean," I panted, nails digging into his shoulders. "I'm—I can't—"

My head fell back, a gasp tearing from my lips as his thumb found my clit—circling once, twice—and the world exploded.

I came hard, crying out against his mouth, my body arching, every nerve alight.

Dean didn't stop—he drove me through it, relentlessly, mercilessly, until the world blurred, and the only thing left was the fire licking through my veins.

I trembled in his arms, shattered and gasping, my pulse hammering against the warm, solid thud of his chest.

When I could finally think again, I looked up—and found his eyes locked on me.

Dark. Steady.

Dangerous in a way I wasn't sure I could survive.

But I didn't want to survive it.

"Dean," I whispered, voice shaking, "I want you."

A guttural sound tore from his throat—raw, desperate—and then his mouth was on mine again, bruising and hungry.

He shifted us, one hand at the back of my neck, the other reaching blindly for his wallet.

I caught the glint of a condom, the smooth foil flashing between us.

Relief—and hunger—spiked through me.

He ripped the package open fast, efficiently, and with urgency, and I could barely breathe as he shoved his jeans and boxers down in one fluid motion.

His cock sprang free—thick, hard—and the sight of him hit me like a jolt of electricity.

He rolled the condom on with shaking fingers.

Then he was lifting me again, my thighs wrapping tight around him, my back against the wall, and—

He thrust into me in one deep, brutal stroke.

The shock punched the air from my lungs, and my body clenched around him, greedy and desperate.

He filled me—every hard, thick inch of him—and the sensation ripped through me, white-hot and blinding.

I gasped, arching into him, the stretch of him making me feel wild, alive, undone.

Dean gritted out a curse against my neck, his hands bruising on my hips, his control fraying with every pulse of my body around him.

"Vivian," he rasped, pulling back and driving into me again until I forgot everything but the feel of him moving inside me.

I clung to him, nails biting into his shoulders, every thrust another breaking point, every gasp another surrender.

"You feel—god, you feel so fucking good," he growled.

"Dean," I sobbed, tightening around him, every nerve raw and exposed.

I didn't care about control. Didn't care about pride.

I just needed him.

"Harder," I begged, breathless. "Fuck me—faster—deeper—harder."

A broken sound tore from his chest—and then he gave me what I wanted.

He drove into me, wild and desperate and glorious, and I met every thrust, gasping, shaking, burning alive under the force of him.

The pressure built again—hot, coiled, unbearable.

"Vivian—" he choked out, voice breaking. "I'm not—Jesus—"

I kissed him, hard and deep, and shattered around him—blinding heat, brilliant white, my body locking down around him as I came, every part of me breaking open in his arms.

Dean groaned my name against my mouth as he followed me over the edge—one last brutal thrust, one last desperate sound—and then he was spilling into the condom, throbbing inside me, his whole body going taut.

He held me through it, body trembling, breath ragged against my skin.

And when the world finally tilted back into focus, he was still there, holding me like he might never let go.

DEAN

I held on to her like a man afraid to let go. Terrified she'd disappear. Afraid this would all turn into a daydream the second I opened my eyes.

I felt her breath catch, and then she let out a soft laugh, and her lips curled unmistakably against mine.

When I opened my eyes, she was smiling—wild and breathless—her hair tumbling around her shoulders, her body still wrapped around mine.

"Christ," I whispered, leaning in until our foreheads touched, her name slipping out like a prayer. "Vivian."

She kissed me—soft, slow, sure. And I knew, in that heartbeat that I would do anything to see her like this again. To keep her.

Then—

"Oh my god," she gasped, pulling back, laughter and horror flashing in her eyes. "Eliza's going to kill us."

I blinked, still lost in the post-apocalyptic haze of *us*. "What?"

"We're supposed to be getting the donation baskets for the fundraiser!" she said, wriggling out of my arms, breathless and half-scandalized. "We've been gone forever!"

A rough, half-formed laugh escaped me as I reluctantly set her down, my hands lingering longer than they should have.

"We should—"

"Get the baskets," she said, smoothing her dress with shaky hands that mirrored my own.

I nodded because words were hard when my pulse was still pounding and my mind was still a mess.

I watched her pull herself back together, thinking about how she'd shattered apart for me just minutes ago. How I already wanted to undo her all over again.

I stepped back and adjusted my clothes because I'd never let her leave this room without another taste if I didn't.

We found the donation baskets neatly packed in boxes in the closet. Between the two of us, we gathered them all and headed out.

She caught my eye as we headed for the truck, sly and smiling, and I barely managed not to drop the damn boxes.

"We're doing that again," she whispered, voice like velvet and wildfire.

The certainty in it—the promise—nearly broke whatever thread of control I had left.

We barely made it into the truck before she tested my resolve again.

Her hand crept over to my thigh—light, teasing—settling there like a dare.

"Vivian," I muttered, meaning it to sound stern. It didn't. It sounded like want.

The look she gave me was sweet, calculated, and anything but innocent. The corner of her mouth twitched like she dared me to call her on it. "What?"

"You know exactly what."

Her fingers slid higher, slow and deliberate, burning through denim.

I gritted my teeth and kept my eyes on the road.

"I'm just being supportive," she said, voice pure sin.

I bit back a groan as her hand climbed higher, a trail of fire against my thigh.

"Community spirit, right?" she added, humming softly like she wasn't about to undo me right here behind the wheel.

"You are going to kill me," I growled, but hell if I didn't want to let her.

She didn't back off. Just watched me with that wicked, knowing smirk that made me want to pull over and fuck her all over again.

"Careful, Counselor," she purred. "You look a little hot under the collar."

I choked out a laugh, half-strangled, clenching the steering wheel like it might save me.

"You're so goddamn dangerous."

She shifted, her palm tracing slow, torturous circles against my thigh, inching closer to my hardening cock and it was a goddamn miracle we didn't crash into a tree.

I was seconds from forgetting how to breathe when we pulled into the parking lot.

She laughed under her breath, pulling her hand away at the last possible second, her breath warm against my jaw.

"Looks like we made it."

"Barely," I rasped, cutting the engine and exhaling like I hadn't taken a full breath since I touched her.

Her eyes sparkled—mischief, satisfaction—and something softer underneath. Something that made it impossible to remember why this was supposed to be a bad idea.

"Good job, Counselor," she said, giving my thigh one last squeeze for good measure.

"Vivian," I warned—low, desperate—but she just grinned and hopped out of the truck.

I followed, grabbing the boxes with shaking hands, my body still vibrating from the memory of hers.

Eliza spotted us halfway across the lot—relieved, wide-eyed, and more than a little suspicious.

"Where have you been?" she demanded, pointing her clipboard at us like a weapon.

"Traffic," I said, straight-faced, shameless.

She narrowed her eyes like she could smell the lie on me.

Vivian just laughed, rich and careless. "I told him to take the scenic route."

Eliza shook her head, half-exasperated. "Well, you made it. Just in time."

"Never doubted us for a second," Vivian said, flashing me a glance so wicked it should've been illegal.

I tried—and probably failed—not to look too pleased. Or too guilty.

Chapter Eight

VIVIAN

We gave Eliza the boxes, and she flashed a grateful smile before scurrying off to finish organizing the auction items.

I stood there, watching Dean, wondering if he felt as breathless and undone as I did. Wondering if he was thinking about how I'd fallen apart in his arms. Wondering if he wanted more.

The look in his eyes told me everything I needed to know.

"Hey, Counselor," I said, voice low and dangerously casual. "Think you could meet me back at my place? I might need some... legal advice."

His gaze snapped to mine, a slow, wicked smile spreading.

"Legal advice," he repeated, the corner of his mouth twitching. "Is that what we're calling it these days?"

"Mmm," I answered, stepping closer, feeling bold, breathless, ready to break every rule I'd ever made. "Very pressing matters."

I let my fingers brush his—light enough to feel like a promise.

"Urgent, even?" he asked, voice rough, full of heat.

"Possibly life or death."

He chuckled, low and devastating, then leaned in, his breath warm against my ear.

"I'll be there."

***

I got to my apartment just before he did. Long enough to do a quick sweep of the place. Long enough to admit that I was utterly, shamelessly gone.

The second I heard the knock, my pulse sprinted. My skin hummed with memory. And God help me—I ached for him.

I opened the door—and there he was.

Eyes locked on mine. Mouth parted—dangerously close, dangerously sure. And every inch of him dared me not to run.

"Counselor," I said, smiling up at him with too much need, "glad you could make it."

"Vivian," he said—and it was a promise.

He pulled me into him, voice low, breath hot against my skin. "How urgent are we talking?"

He kicked the door shut behind him—and then his mouth was on mine. Hot. Hungry. Devastating.

By the time he pulled away, we were both breathless, clinging.

"Tell me if this is too much," he rasped, his hands cradling my face, searching my eyes. "Tell me if you need me to back off."

I laughed—a wild, broken sound. "Dean. If you back off, I might die."

He groaned—a rough, desperate sound—and kissed me again, fierce and consuming.

Backing me toward the bedroom. Dragging me under all over again.

We barely made it to the mattress.

He stripped my sundress over my head, kissing down the curve of my neck. Every graze of his lips set my skin on fire.

I tugged at his T-shirt, frantic to feel him, finally yanking it over his head and drinking him in—broad shoulders, lean muscle, the kind of body that begged for hands, lips, and reckless decisions.

He watched me shimmy out of my panties, his eyes darkening, his jaw going tight. I hooked my thumbs into his waistband and pulled him down to me—the weight of him grounding, electrifying.

"This time," he murmured against my mouth, "I'm taking my time."

He cupped my breasts, thumbs grazing over my nipples through my bra, and I arched into his touch, aching for more.

He unclasped it with a slow flick of his fingers, and when the lace slipped away, the look in his eyes made me shiver.

He lowered his mouth to my nipple and sucked deeply. Each long, deliberate pull created an intense, aching sensation that ignited sparks in my body and left my pussy drenched with desire.

I tugged at his hair, desperate for more, but he only chuckled—low, wicked.

"Impatient, Vivian?"

"Yes," I gasped, shameless. "God, yes."

He just smiled, dangerous and knowing. Reading me far too well, he caught my wrist when my hand drifted down, desperate for friction.

"Uh-uh," he said, voice a dark caress. "Not yet."

I whimpered—a sound I'd never made before—and he kissed a path lower, lower, every inch of my skin a live wire.

"Patience is overrated," I panted, arching into him.

He only smiled again—and pinned my wrists over my head with one hand. I nearly came undone right then.

He took his time until I was trembling, begging, panting his name.

"Please," I whispered, desperate.

He groaned, voice thick with want. "God, I love the way you say that."

"Then stop teasing—"

His mouth finally reached my core, and the world narrowed down to the exquisite sensation of his lips and tongue, exploring every intimate curve and contour of my pussy.

His tongue moved slowly, deliberately, relentlessly. I bucked against him, gasping, and crying out with every flick, every stroke.

When he slid two fingers inside me—perfect, sure, deep—I broke apart. Shattered. Came so hard that the world turned white around the edges.

He didn't stop until I was whispering his name like a prayer.

I pulled him up to me, kissing him hard—wild and wanting and desperate. His hands were already at his waist, shoving down his pants and boxers in one rough motion. I fumbled blindly for the nightstand, finding the condom by touch.

He groaned when I tore it open, a sound so rough I felt it everywhere.

"Hurry," he begged against my mouth.

I rolled it over him, feeling him thick and hard and trembling with restraint.

Then he thrust into me—deep, sudden—and the shock of it made me cry out, arching against him.

He filled me completely, perfectly, the stretch of him igniting every nerve; every place I'd forgotten could feel this good.

DEAN

It was like the first time—Wild. Consuming. No room to breathe. No room to think.

Only better.

I pulled her closer, my mouth open against her skin, my hands gripping her hips like I might lose my mind if I let go. She moved under me, with me, her body arching, her breath coming in ragged, desperate gasps—and I was already a lost cause. Already so deep inside her, I could barely breathe.

Her legs locked around my waist, and I drove into her, every rough stroke pushing us closer to the edge.

I couldn't stop.

Couldn't hold back.

Couldn't do anything but give in to the wild, reckless rhythm she pulled from me.

She gasped my name—a breathless, broken sound—and I felt her tighten around me, slick and hot and impossibly tight.

The edge slammed into me, rushing up fast and brutal, and I didn't fight it.

"Vivian," I groaned, my voice breaking apart as my body shuddered, feeling every ripple, every tight, wet clench, my vision blurring as I came with a raw, staggering force. Everything else fell away until there was only her—and this.

We stayed tangled until the world finally slid back into focus—until I could see the curve of her mouth, the flush across her skin, and the impossible, breathtaking reality of her.

I eased back carefully, and she let out a low, satisfied sound—a sound that hit me harder than any orgasm ever could.

She smiled—wild and wicked and beautiful—and I knew right then I was absolutely hers.

"We're doing that again," she said—same words, same grin, but this time it wasn't a dare. It was a promise.

A laugh tore out of me—rough, unsteady, real. "Yeah, we are."

Vivian shifted, her hair spilling across the pillow, her body still impossibly close to mine.

"Think you can keep up, Counselor?" she teased, arching a brow.

I met her gaze, steady and unflinching. "You have no idea."

She kissed me—slow and deep—and I felt my body respond before I could catch my breath.

Christ. Again?

I groaned into her mouth, barely hanging onto my sanity.

"Vivian," I muttered, pulling back just enough to breathe, "you're going to be the death of me."

Her fingers trailed down my stomach, feather-light, teasing.

"Looks like you're still alive, Counselor." Her voice was pure velvet—and pure sin. "And just as eager as the first time."

A rough sound escaped me—half disbelief, half desperation—as she wrapped her hand around my cock and started stroking.

She grinned, wicked and unrepentant.

"Unless," she teased, her hand sliding lower, fingers wrapping around my balls, "you need a break?"

I growled low in my throat—and flipped her over onto her stomach.

I dragged her up onto her knees, moving in close behind her, unable to stop myself even if I'd tried.

I didn't know how she made me feel like this—how she made me feel like a twenty-year-old again, hard and aching and ready to lose my damn mind.

I grabbed another condom, tearing it open with shaking hands, barely holding on.

Vivian rubbed back against me—hot, desperate—and I nearly lost it right there.

I groaned and slid the condom on quickly.

She looked over her shoulder, eyes locking with mine—and whatever I thought I knew about control shattered. Because the look in her eyes? It leveled me.

I thrust into her deep and hard—and the jolt of it hit us both.

She cried out—high, needy—and her body clamped down around me again, slick and tight and impossibly good.

I tangled my fingers in her hair, pulling just enough to make her gasp.

God, she was perfect. Wild and desperate and so fucking beautiful I couldn't breathe.

She let out a ragged moan—and I gave up holding anything back.

I drove into her—faster, harder—my body crashing into hers, every thrust pushing us closer to the edge.

"Dean," she gasped, desperate and wild. "Don't—don't stop—"

No chance in hell.

I held on, barely hanging together, feeling her tremble, feeling everything coiling, winding tighter.

One more thrust—

She cried out, her body clenching around me, and I lost it.

I slammed into her deep and hard one last time, letting the orgasm tear through me—wild, brutal, blinding.

We came together—

A riot of sound.

A rush of heat.

A breaking apart so completely I didn't know where she ended, and I began.

We collapsed onto the bed—tangled, shaking.

I eased out of her slowly, carefully, every nerve humming, and pulled her into my arms.

I didn't care that my muscles felt shot. Didn't care that the room was still spinning.

I only cared about the way she smiled up at me.

Chapter Nine

VIVIAN

The sun was just starting to seep through the blinds when I woke.

Dean was still asleep beside me — warm, steady, his arm slung over my waist like he belonged there.

I froze, heart stuttering.

I was sure I looked like a mess. My hair was tangled, my makeup smudged, and I had none of the polish I usually wore like a shield.

This wasn't the version of me men usually wanted.

I slid out of bed carefully, barely breathing, and tiptoed to the bathroom, shutting the door softly.

Staring at my reflection, my stomach twisted.

No armor. No safety net. No curated version of myself to hide behind.

Just... Vivian.

I splashed water on my face, scrubbing away the remnants of the night. Trying—desperately—to find something polished in the mirror. Something he could still want.

When I opened the door, the towel pressed to my face; I wasn't expecting him to be awake.

But he was.

Sitting up against the headboard, sheet slung low across his hips, dark eyes locked on me.

Wide awake.

And seeing everything.

"Morning, beautiful," he said, voice rough with sleep.

I froze.

Because there was no hiding now.

He smiled, slow and steady—like seeing me like this wasn't a shock. Like I didn't need my armor.

I felt the panic rise—fast, brutal—clawing up my throat before I could stop it.

"You don't have to say that," I said, voice tight.

Dean frowned. "Say what?"

"That I'm beautiful."

He blinked, brow furrowing like I'd just spoken a different language. "I'm not saying it because I have to."

His gaze held mine, unflinching. Like the truth had just settled between us, and he wasn't backing down. "Vivian—"

"Don't," I said quietly, the words slipping out as I took a small step back, unable to stop myself.

Confusion flickered across his face, along with hurt.

But the instinct to protect myself slammed into place before I could stop it.

"I have a lot to do today," I said, voice high and bright and false. "You should probably—"

I gestured vaguely toward the door, hating myself more with every word.

He wasn't angry—just quiet, with a sadness in his eyes that made it harder to breathe.

"Okay," he said, voice low and steady. "If that's what you want."

It wasn't. God, it wasn't.

I tightened my grip on the towel, stepped aside, and let him gather his things.

And when the door clicked shut behind him, I finally let myself sink to the floor, pressing my hands to my face—

hating that I'd written the ending I'd feared the most and still felt like I didn't have a choice. Because it always ended the same.

They see the real you.

And then they leave.

***

I sat there, staring at the empty space where Dean had been.

The way the sunlight slanted through the blinds. The rumpled sheets. The fragile pieces of a morning that could've been something different.

If I weren't... me.

If I weren't so good at ruining things before they had the chance to ruin me.

My hand moved without thinking, fumbling for my phone like it might anchor me.

I didn't even realize I'd called Veronica until she answered.

"Viv? What's wrong?"

My throat closed up. I almost hung up. Almost lied.

But something cracked open instead.

"I kicked him out," I said, my voice small and raw.

"Dean?" she said carefully.

I squeezed my eyes shut. "He saw me. All of me. No makeup, no armor. Just... me."

Veronica's voice dropped, softer now. "And?"

"And he didn't run." The words ripped out of me. "I did."

I heard her exhale—slow, steady. "Oh, Viv."

"I couldn't—" My voice broke. I pressed a hand to my forehead. "He said I was beautiful. Like he meant it. And I couldn't believe him. I couldn't... I couldn't let him be the one to leave."

Veronica didn't say anything at first.

When she did, her voice was gentler than I'd ever heard.

"I didn't realize it went that deep for you," she said. "The armor. The needing to be perfect."

I let out a choked sound that wasn't quite a laugh. "It's always been that deep."

"I'm sorry," she said quietly. "I thought... I thought you wore it because you liked it. The polish. The control."

"I do," I whispered. "But it's not just that."

"I know," she said. "I see it now."

Veronica's voice was low but fierce. "You don't need the armor, Viv. You never really did, not with him."

I shook my head, even though she couldn't see me. "He's going to realize I'm not perfect. And he's going to leave."

She laughed—a soft sound that cracked something open in me. "Vivian. He already knows you're not perfect. None of us are. And he stayed anyway."

I closed my eyes, the ache in my chest splintering wide open.

"He's not our father," Veronica said, her voice fierce with conviction. "This isn't *that* story."

I didn't answer. Couldn't.

"Let yourself be loved," she said. "You don't have to be flawless."

The tears spilled over then—silent, furious.

Because some part of me wanted so badly to believe her.

Wanted so badly to believe him.

"I'm scared," I whispered.

"I know," she said, steady as ever. "But maybe that's how you know it's real."

I stayed there on the floor long after we hung up.

Stayed until the light shifted.

Until the apartment grew small around me.

I'd spent so long guarding myself with solitude—telling myself I didn't need more or deserve more.

But the thought of losing him?

That was the first thing that ever made me question the lie.

DEAN

I drove around for a while after leaving her apartment.

No destination. No plan. Just me—and the silence that made it impossible to lie to myself.

I kept replaying it in my head—how she looked when she pushed me away. Not angry. Not cold. Just... scared.

And somehow, that left a deeper mark than anything she could've said.

I should've been angry. I meant every word, every look—and she still didn't trust it. Didn't trust me.

But I wasn't angry. I was hollow. Confused. And still—God help me—certain.

Because what I saw in her eyes wasn't rejection.

It was fear.

And beneath that? Hope. Small. Fragile. Beating like a trapped bird in her chest.

She thought pushing me away would hurt less than letting me stay.

Thought giving me an out would save her from the heartbreak she believed was coming.

Hadn't she realized it yet? I was already all in. Already too far gone.

I gripped the steering wheel tighter, my pulse pounding harder the longer I sat with it.

I didn't know when it had happened. When she got under my skin, into my blood—became the one person I didn't want to live without.

Maybe it was that day at the diner.

Or when she smiled like she dared the world to hurt her.

Or looked at me like she didn't believe in miracles... but was willing to risk it anyway.

It didn't matter when it happened or how. All I knew was that whatever this was between us was real. And real was worth fighting for. I wasn't walking away from her, from this... not even if she tried to give me a hundred reasons to.

She deserved someone who didn't scare easy. Someone who stayed. Someone who could look at every sharp, broken, brilliant part of her and choose her anyway.

And I was damn sure that someone was me.

I flicked my blinker on and made a hard U-turn.

Because this wasn't over. Not by a long shot.

***

I didn't bother texting. Didn't call. I wasn't giving her the chance to close the door before I even knocked.

I just parked, climbed the stairs two at a time, and knocked.

Stillness wrapped around me, but under my skin, everything raced. The air felt tight like it was holding its breath—waiting, just like me. I could almost feel her on the other side of the door, her heartbeat quick, her hand hovering near the handle, deciding whether to let me in or let fear win.

I knocked again. Softer this time.

"Vivian," I said, voice low, steady. "I'm not here to push. Or fight. I'm just... here."

Still nothing.

I scrubbed a hand over my jaw, my heart hammering harder than it had any right to.

"I'm not leaving," I said, leaning my forehead against the door. "Not unless you look me in the eye and tell me this—*us*—meant nothing to you."

The lock clicked, the door eased open—and there she was, stripped of all her armor and still, somehow, the most stunning woman I'd ever seen.

I stepped inside, closing the door softly behind me.

The air between us buzzed with all the things we hadn't said. All the fear. All the wanting. All the hope.

I stayed a few feet back. Gave her room.

"I'm not here to make this harder," I said, voice rough. "I'm here because you're scared. And I'm not."

She opened her mouth—probably to argue or lie—but I shook my head.

"Don't," I said, voice low. "Don't tell me it didn't mean anything. I know fear when I see it, Vivian—but I also know what it feels like when something's real. And this... this is real.

Vivian looked away, her voice barely above a whisper. "I spent a long time thinking I had to be perfect. That if I wasn't... people would leave."

I took a step closer, slow and steady. "I'm not going anywhere."

"You should hate me," she whispered, broken.

"I don't," I said simply.

"You should leave."

"I'm not going anywhere," I repeated.

Her breath hitched. Her eyes shimmered, wide and raw.

"I'm scared," she said so quietly it almost broke me.

I stepped closer. Close enough to reach her if she let me.

"I'm not," I said, my voice catching. "You don't scare me, *this* doesn't scare me."

Her eyes flooded, but she didn't look away.

"I'm not perfect, Vivian," I said, softer now. "You're not either. That's not what this is about."

She stared at me like I was offering her something she didn't know she was allowed to want.

So I said it: "You don't have to be perfect to be loved."

The first tear slipped down her cheek.

Then another.

I closed the distance between us, lifted my hand—slow, careful—and brushed the tears away with my thumb.

She shuddered under the touch but didn't pull back.

"I see you," I said, voice breaking. "All of you. And I'm still right here."

For a long, gut-wrenching moment, she just stared at me.

Then—like she was stepping off the edge of a cliff—she reached for me.

Wrapped her arms around my waist. Buried her face in my chest. And let herself fall.

I caught her. Held her tight.

Tangled my fingers in her hair and breathed her in.

And when she whispered my name against my heart, I knew she wasn't running. And I wasn't letting go.

Epilogue

VIVIAN

6 months later

The Velvet Room had settled into its version of quiet—just the low hum of exit lights, the soft clink of glass behind the bar, and the hush that followed a night of music and noise.

I grabbed my jacket from backstage, already spinning tomorrow's rehearsal schedule through my mind.

Dean was leaning by the door, watching me with that steady, impossible gaze that still made my chest ache in ways I wasn't used to.

"You ready?" he asked, voice low.

"Almost." I slung the jacket over my arm and returned to the bar to grab my keys.

That's when I heard it — the soft creak of the stage stairs.

I looked up, frowning—only to see him climbing the stairs like he belonged there. Like the spotlight didn't faze him. Like this was precisely where he was meant to be.

He stepped into the low pool of light at center stage—no music, no script, just him. Dean was standing there with nerves in his eyes, but his shoulders were squared like he wasn't going anywhere. "I don't have a routine," he said, voice rough with something that hit me square in the chest. "No velvet. No feather. No smoke and mirrors."

I swallowed hard, my heart climbing higher with every word.

"All I've got is this," he said. He held his arms out slightly — open, bare, unguarded. "Me. The guy who's stupidly, hopelessly in love with you."

The world tilted. Tilted and steadied and came into sharper focus than it ever had before.

Dean smiled—quiet, sure, like giving me his heart was the easiest thing he'd ever done. And it took every breath I had not to fall apart.

I did the only thing that made sense. I dropped my jacket, every last fear, every broken story I used to tell myself about love, leaving, and loss, and I ran.

Ran down the aisle, up the stairs, across the stage, straight to him.

Dean met me halfway.

I launched myself into his arms and kissed him hard, fierce, shameless. He caught me like he always had — strong, steady, and sure — and kissed me back like he'd been waiting his whole life for it.

When we finally broke apart, I leaned in, brushing my mouth against his. "Took you long enough, Counselor."

He laughed—soft, low, and so full of love it made my chest ache.

He cupped the back of my neck, his forehead resting against mine.

"I love you," he whispered.

And I believed him.

And I knew I wasn't alone anymore.

Not ever again.

***

Dear Reader,

Thank you so much for reading *Silk & Silence*—and for stepping into the guarded hearts of Vivian and Dean with me.

This story was built on walls: the kind we build to survive, to protect, to keep love at a distance. But it's also about what happens when someone finally sees through the cracks—and chooses to stay.

Vivian's control, Dean's quiet armor, and the slow unraveling of everything they thought they needed to stay safe made this one of the most tender, vulnerable books I've ever written. I hope their journey reminded you that being seen—truly seen—can be the bravest kind of love.

If *Silk & Silence* made you swoon, sigh, or feel a little less alone, I'd be so grateful if you left a review. Every review helps new readers discover the series and supports stories that center flawed, fierce, and deeply human love. You can review the book here.

The Thorne sisters still have stories to tell—and I promise they're just getting started.

With all my love,
Hana York

***

Pleasure & Prose

A steamy, small-town opposites-attract romance between a buttoned-up professor and the most unexpected woman he's ever desired

Hana York

Pink Pop Publishing

Pleasure & Prose

(The Thorne Sisters Book 3)

Copyright © 2025 by Hana York

www.HanaYork.com

Contents

Prologue

VERONICA

Pleasure & Co. was steady this afternoon.

I leaned a hip against the counter, arms folded, watching women move through the aisles with easy certainty.

They compared options, read labels, and asked questions without embarrassment.

Toys. Accessories. A few racks of lingerie along the back wall.

Not the heart of the shop, but a nice touch.

People liked to categorize places like mine.

Places where women could be themselves.

Where they could live, love, and learn without shame.

Where they could own their bodies, and their pleasure, without asking permission.

That made some people uncomfortable.

The idea that women didn't need to be told what was acceptable.

That they could want more, take more, *be* more, and not apologize for any of it.

It was easier to pretend this place was reckless.

That the women who came here were desperate. Or broken. Or sad.

Anything to avoid admitting the truth: These women were free.

And they didn't need anyone's approval to stay that way.

The bell above the door chimed.

I looked up, expecting another woman ready to take what she needed without apology.

Instead, a man stood just inside the entrance, looking like he wasn't sure he was allowed to be here.

Tall. Lean. Rumpled brown hair. Tortoise shell glasses.

A tweed jacket that had seen too many dry cleanings.

The kind of man who belonged behind a stack of books, not under the soft glow of Pleasure & Co.'s lights.

Attractive, despite the nerves practically rolling off him.

Maybe even because of them.

He took one wide-eyed look around and stiffened, like he'd just realized he was hopelessly out of place.

Our eyes met.

He straightened his jacket, shoved his hands into his pockets, and started toward the counter with the grim determination of a man walking into traffic.

A slow smile tugged at the corner of my mouth.

My day just got a lot more interesting.

Chapter One

SIMON

I was lost.

Hopelessly, embarrassingly lost.

The directions to Paper Moon Bookshop were still sitting neatly on the bureau at my flat.

I'd been so sure I wouldn't need them.

After all, how hard could it be to find a bookshop in a town this size?

Impossible apparently.

Briar Hill was not laid out sensibly.

Or perhaps it was, and my English instincts refused to cooperate.

Either way, I'd been walking in circles for fifteen minutes and was dangerously close to being late.

I scanned the street for anything that looked remotely bookish.

A florist—closed.

A café—boarded up for renovations.

An antique shop—lights off, sign flipped to *Sorry, We're Closed*.

And then—*Pleasure & Co.*

The only shop open.

The only option.

I stopped dead in my tracks.

Modest gold lettering marked the window, light from within casting a soft gleam across the glass.

Inside, warm hues and velvet displays hinted at a world I had no business stepping into.

Absolutely not the bookshop.

Still... a shop was a shop.

Someone inside might give me directions.

Preferably before I lost what little dignity I had left.

I pushed the door open before I could talk myself out of it.

A soft chime rang above me, and warm air wrapped around my shoulders like a trap.

Velvet displays. Glass cases glowing under low, inviting lights.

And shelves lined with objects I absolutely was not prepared to encounter in public.

I tried not to stare at any item too long, fearing the comparison might not be flattering.

Movement behind the counter caught my eye.

A woman.

She stood with one hip cocked, arms folded across a silky raspberry blouse, watching me with a calm, unreadable expression.

Dark hair tucked behind one ear. Sharp mouth painted a deep berry color.

Poised. Elegant. Entirely unbothered by the absurdity of my presence.

Our eyes met and I forgot, briefly, why I was there at all.

There was nothing shy about her. Nothing hesitant or uncertain.

She seemed entirely comfortable in her skin, something I'd spent most of my life quietly wishing I could be.

The heat rising up the back of my neck had nothing to do with the temperature.

I straightened my jacket, shoved my hands into my pockets, and walked toward her.

She didn't smile.

She just watched, like someone studying a fish out of water.

I had the distinct feeling I was making a memorable first impression.

Words.

I needed words.

Preferably not the ones scrambling through my mind like startled livestock.

"Good afternoon."

Polite. Neutral. Safe.

I opened my mouth and immediately forgot how to be a functioning member of society.

Because of course, only a madman would walk into a shop like this and start with *good afternoon*, as if browsing vibrators and blindfolds were a standard part of one's day.

Brilliant, Radcliffe. Absolutely brilliant.

I cleared my throat, resisting the overwhelming urge to flee.

"Forgive me," I managed, voice a beat too stiff. "I'm terribly sorry to bother you, but I seem to have lost my way."

Lost my way.

In a shop like this.

Outstanding.

It was, by all accounts, not my finest hour.

VERONICA

He wasn't the first man to wander into Pleasure & Co. looking lost.

But he might've been the first who didn't wear his discomfort like a joke.

No smirk. No leering glance.

Just that stiff posture and polite desperation, like he'd rather be anywhere else, and couldn't bring himself to be rude about it.

Interesting. Unexpected.

Most men who walked in here had a confident swagger.

Like the sheer act of crossing the threshold made them bold and entitled.

They saw the window displays, the velvet chairs, the curated toys, and assumed they understood.

But not him.

There was no performance in the way he stood there, fidgeting awkwardly.

No calculation in the way his gaze skated carefully over the displays.

He wasn't pretending to be at ease.

He wasn't pretending at all.

And somehow, that was more magnetic than any polished charm or empty promise had ever been. I kept my expression neutral, resting one hand lightly on the counter.

He shifted slightly, unsure if he was meant to speak or melt into the floor.

I stayed exactly where I was, letting the silence stretch.

If he wanted something, he'd have to find the words himself.

He cleared his throat.

"Forgive me," he said, each word crisp and deliberate.

"I seem to have lost my way. I'm looking for the Paper Moon Bookshop. Would you happen to know where it is?"

His unmistakable English accent made even getting lost sound dignified.

Maybe that explained his stiffness. Or, maybe not.

Either way, it made him even more interesting.

Something about him, something in the way he stood there, all earnest discomfort and ironclad politeness, made me want to see what might be hiding under all that careful restraint.

The pull was instant.

Sharp.

Unavoidable.

I tucked a strand of hair behind my ear and offered the smooth, practiced smile I usually reserved for nervous first-time buyers.

"Two blocks down," I said. "Hang a right at the coffee shop with the green awning. You can't miss it."

Relief flickered across his face.

He nodded, murmured a quiet, "Thank you," and turned to go.

And just like that, I knew I wasn't ready to let him.

"Actually," I said lightly, before he reached the door, "I'm heading that way myself. I've got a delivery for the owner. I'm Veronica Thorne, by the way, owner of Pleasure & Co."

He hesitated, clearly unsure whether he was supposed to accept or if saying yes would somehow violate a rule only he knew.

"Simon Radcliffe," he said, voice polite but uncertain. "I teach at the university."

I tucked another strand of hair behind my ear, letting a small smile curl my mouth.

"Relax," I added, voice low and dry.

"I don't bite, unless asked nicely."

That earned me the smallest huff of laughter.

A warm flicker of satisfaction curled in my chest, sharper than I expected.

God, it had been a long time since teasing someone felt this good.

"I'll just be a second," I said, nodding toward the back.

He gave a short, awkward nod and stayed put.

I slipped through the curtain, grabbed the slim brown package off the shipping shelf, and returned a moment later.

He was exactly where I'd left him, hands in his pockets doing his best not to look at anything too closely.

When he caught sight of me, he straightened.

Flushed, just a little.

Adorable.

Without a word, he stepped aside, falling into step as I crossed the room.

At the door, he moved ahead just enough to reach it first, pulling it open with stiff, careful politeness.

Chivalrous to the bone.

The kind of man who held doors, not to be noticed, but because it was wired into him.

Dangerous, that kind of decency.

The kind that could undo a woman if she wasn't careful.

And I wasn't in the business of being undone.

I stepped past him into the sunlight, the package tucked under my arm, and felt his presence hover close behind me, like he still wasn't sure he belonged at my side.

I wasn't sure either.

But I knew better than to underestimate the pull of curiosity, my kryptonite.

Chapter Two

SIMON

I should have declined.

Politely, of course.

A thank-you, a murmur of gratitude, then a swift retreat into the crooked maze of Briar Hill's streets.

Instead, I walked beside her, matching her stride with the stiff, awkwardness of a man painfully aware he was out of his depth.

She moved like honey warmed by the afternoon sun, slow, sure, and impossible to look away from.

No hesitation. No careful hedging of space.

She existed like the world had learned it was easier to make room than deny her.

It was, God help me, beautiful.

I should have kept my head down. Focused on the sidewalk like a sensible man.

Instead, I stole glances.

Brief, helpless things that only tightened the ache in my chest.

I shouldn't have been looking at her.

Shouldn't have been *thinking* about her the way I was.

But she made it impossible, simply by being real in a way I'd never quite learned how to be.

She caught me looking, of course.

Not directly, she was too gracious for that, but the flicker at the corner of her mouth gave me away.

I cleared my throat, desperate to salvage a shred of dignity.

"I hope this isn't... an imposition," I managed, already wincing at how stiff I sounded.

She slanted me a look, warm and knowing.

"Relax. You didn't kidnap me. I volunteered."

I stumbled over absolutely nothing.

Brilliant.

"Much appreciated," I muttered, earning the slightest curl of a smile.

The kind that felt like a secret slipped just beneath my skin.

We turned the corner, and the bookshop appeared, a narrow brick storefront with a hand-painted sign swinging above the door.

She adjusted the package under her arm, steps easy and unhurried.

I knew I was running out of time.

In a few minutes, she'd hand over the delivery, murmur something polite, and vanish back into a world I had no place in.

I cleared my throat and words scraped their way up from somewhere I usually kept locked tight.

"I'm actually meant to lecture here in a few minutes," I said, meeting her eyes. "But... if you're free later, I'd love to buy you a tea."

The words hung there, awkward and exposed.

Of course she would decline.

Of course she had better things to do than humor a flustered academic who couldn't even find a bookshop.

She regarded me for a moment, steady, unreadable.

Then the corner of her mouth curved.

"Pleasure & Co. closes at six," she said, voice smooth as velvet. "If you're serious, you'll find me there."

The breath I hadn't realized I was holding slipped out in a rush.

Serious.

God, if only she knew.

***

The lecture passed in a blur.

Polite questions. Applause. A few earnest conversations I barely heard.

I left as soon as possible, the sheaf of notes trembling slightly in my hands.

The walk back to Pleasure & Co. felt longer than it should have.

I'd known attraction before—the careful, manageable kind.

Polite admiration. Staid affection.

The sort of feeling you could tuck into a dinner conversation and forget by dessert.

But this?

This was raw. Unruly.

I wanted her in ways I didn't have a vocabulary for.

The kind of wanting that made my fingers twitch with the need to touch, to hold, to feel the proof of her against me, in the most wildly, hopelessly respectable way imaginable.

It shocked me.

How badly I wanted her.

How *right* it felt.

It was as if some long-buried part of myself, buried under years of good manners and cautious half-living, had finally cracked open.

I had no idea what to do with it.

No idea how to be a man she might desire.

But walking away?

Letting this slip through my fingers?

That, I couldn't stomach.

The sky had deepened, the air cooling against the back of my neck as I reached Pleasure & Co.

The windows glowed warm against the dusk, a beacon against everything safe and cautious I had ever been.

I stopped just shy of the door, heart hammering.

For one ridiculous second, I thought about turning back.

Pretending this had all been a moment of madness.

But then I remembered the way she said it—matter-of-fact, not teasing: *If you're serious, you'll find me there.*

I was serious.

God help me. I was serious in ways that scared the life out of me.

I pulled in a breath.

Straightened my jacket.

And pushed open the door.

VERONICA

The late afternoon light stretched across the pavement, painting everything in gold and shadow as I returned to Pleasure & Co.

The package had been dropped off without fanfare — a quick word with the owner of the Paper Moon, a polite thanks, and I was free.

But my mind wasn't.

It circled back to the man I'd left at the bookshop.

Professor Simon Radcliffe.

All politeness and careful words, like too much honesty might send the world spinning.

On the surface, he was everything my younger self might've rolled her eyes at.

Tweed. Glasses. Posture so stiff it was a wonder he didn't creak when he walked.

But beneath all that careful armor...

There was something else.

A flicker of rawness in his eyes.

A restless energy he didn't know how to channel.

It made me wonder, not just about the man he showed the world, but about the one he tried so hard to hide.

Was he all neat lines and restrained smiles?

Or was there something more profound, something rougher, wilder?

The kind of man who might shove a woman against a wall and kiss her breathless, then stammer out an apology afterward.

I smiled to myself, shaking my head.

Ridiculous.

He'd probably be too polite to even think about it.

And yet—

A thread of curiosity tugged tight inside me.

And I didn't want to cut it loose.

I pushed open the door to Pleasure & Co., the familiar chime pulling me back to reality.

The shop was steady, a few customers browsing, and low music humming in the air.

Normal.

Predictable.

But everything in me buzzed with restless energy.

I slipped behind the counter, checking the time, and swore under my breath.

Dinner.

Vivian's house. Takeout. Wine. Sisters.

I was supposed to be there in less than an hour.

I leaned on the counter, head dipping forward as I muttered a string of creative curses.

Of course I'd forgotten.

Of course today, of all days, I'd let myself get distracted.

I pulled out my phone, pulled up our group chat and typed: *Something came up. Can't make it tonight. Sorry.*

Vivian: *Define "something."*

Lola: *I bet that "something" comes with a six-pack and a brooding stare.*

Vivian: *I WANT DETAILS NOW.*

Eliza: *Just be safe, okay? We'll save you leftovers.*

Lola: *If you don't tell us in the next thirty seconds, I'm showing up at your place with popcorn.*

Vivian: *And wine. And judgment.*

I sighed, knowing exactly how this would escalate.

Typed back: *I did someone a favor. They offered to buy me tea. That's it. Relax.*

The responses came fast:

Vivian: *Tea? He'd better be hot if you're suffering through tea.*

Lola: *You mean like a Long Island Iced Tea, right??? Otherwise, WHAT ARE WE EVEN DOING?*

Eliza: *That sounds very nice. Can't wait to hear all about it!*

I shook my head, smiling despite myself.

I muted the thread buying myself maybe ten minutes of peace.

Maybe.

I turned back toward the door just as it swung open and there he was.

Simon Radcliffe.

A little rumpled. A little flushed.

But steady.

His shoulders squared, no frantic glances toward the exit.

No fidgeting.

He crossed the room with quiet purpose.

I straightened behind the counter, a flicker of warmth curling low in my stomach.

He stopped a few feet inside, meeting my eyes without flinching.

"I hope I'm not too late," he said. "You did say six."

I let the corner of my mouth curve. "Right on time."

I stepped out from behind the counter.

He stood directly in my path.

I meant to skirt around him.

Gracefully.

Instead, my hip brushed his side, and instinctively, his hand shot out to steady me.

Just fingertips at my waist.

Barely a touch.

But the jolt that shot through me? Lightening.

My breath hitched.

His hand dropped, fingers flexing slightly before he pulled away.

Neither of us said anything.

I flipped the *OPEN* sign to *CLOSED*, praying he hadn't noticed how my fingers trembled.

When I turned back, he stood politely trying to look comfortable when he clearly wasn't.

It tugged at something in me, something protective and amused.

"Come on, Professor," I said lightly. "Before you sprain something trying not to make eye contact, let me grab my things. There's a café around the corner with slightly less...distracting decor."

I was halfway behind the counter when his voice stopped me.

"Wait."

I turned, one brow arched.

He cleared his throat, shifting slightly, every movement careful.

"I'm sure it's obvious," he said, a small, rueful smile tugging at his mouth, "but... this isn't exactly my comfort zone."

He ruffled his hair, making it worse.

"But that's my hang-up. Not yours."

Something in my chest softened.

"And yet," he added, almost sheepish, "hazard of being an academic, I suppose. When I don't understand something, I want to."

I leaned a hip against the counter, studying him.

This man who felt wildly out of place—but still wanted to stay.

Wanted to understand.

Wanted to *see*.

"What do you want to know?" I asked, my voice even.

He shifted closer without realizing it, hands tucked in his jacket pockets.

"Why did you open it?" he said simply. "Why does it matter to you?"

Chapter Three

VERONICA

I wasn't used to being asked.

Not like this.

Not without judgment tucked behind curiosity, or condescension wrapped in a smile.

Just a question—simple, direct, and sincere.

It shouldn't have thrown me.

But it did.

I could've brushed him off.

Made a joke. Sent him on his way.

But something in his expression, so open, so rare, made me want to answer.

Really answer.

"This shop," I said, "is about giving women space to be themselves. To own their bodies. To explore what they want—without apology, without shame."

Simon's eyes stayed locked on mine. Not flinching. Not retreating.

"It's about teaching women that pleasure isn't something they have to justify. That they don't need permission to want more. To take more. To *be* more."

I let the truth hang there.

"Most of the world still wants women to be small," I said. "To live within the lines someone else drew for them."

I shook my head. "This place isn't about fantasy. It isn't about performance. It's about freedom. Claiming every part of yourself—every hunger, every curiosity, every joy—and refusing to be ashamed of it."

The words stretched between us like a living thing.

Simon didn't speak right away. He just looked at me, like he was seeing something he didn't know he'd been starving for until now.

When he finally spoke, his voice was rough around the edges.

"I think..." he said slowly, "that's one of the bravest, most necessary things I've ever heard."

I held his gaze.

And for the first time in a long time I felt seen.

Not as a performance. Not as a provocation.

Just... seen.

By a man who didn't know a damn thing about me and still saw more than most ever had.

Simon still didn't look away, even as the silence stretched between us like a wire pulled tight.

When he spoke again, his voice was soft. Careful.

"I didn't grow up in a family that talked about... things like this. Not intimacy. Not emotion. Not... anything that risked cracking the surface."

I didn't speak.

Something was opening behind his words.

"We weren't cold, exactly. Just... tidy. Everything in its place. Especially feelings."

His mouth twitched. Not quite a smile.

"I learned to admire from a distance. To want quietly, if at all."

He exhaled.

"But you... You don't worry about propriety. Or what anyone thinks you *should* be."

The look in his eyes was raw. Unshielded.

Nothing like the man who'd walked into my shop, terrified of his own desire.

"It's unsettling," he said finally. "And..."

A tremor caught his voice.

"Remarkable."

I didn't breathe.

"And I want to understand it," he added, the words tumbling out. "I want to understand *you*. I want..."

He stopped, a flush rising to his cheeks.

Eyes dropping. Shoulders hunching.

"I'm sorry. I'm not very good at this."

He was closer than he'd been all evening.

Close enough to see the pulse fluttering at his throat.

"I think you're better than you know," I said softly.

I saw the words land, saw his tension ease, just a little.

I wanted to reach for him.

To close the distance, for his sake as much as mine.

I wanted to know what else might be waiting beneath the surface.

"Come on, Professor. Let's get out of here before I decide you're too good to be true."

He held the door for me, his hand brushing the small of my back as I passed.

I felt it everywhere.

An invitation.

A promise.

A risk I wasn't sure I knew how to take.

But I had a feeling he'd make me remember.

SIMON

I had no idea what I was doing.

Veronica walked beside me, close enough to touch, and all I could think was how wildly out of my league I was.

This was not the plan.

I was supposed to be sensible. Respectful. In control.

But I could feel that control slipping, fraying at the edges like my pulse.

I needed a script. A plan.

I needed to stop wanting her so badly I could barely breathe.

She was everything I wasn't.

Direct. Passionate. Unafraid.

She didn't just know herself. She owned it.

And God help me, I wanted to understand her, too.

Really know her, in ways I didn't have words for—ways I'd never let myself contemplate before.

The café was quiet, half-empty, the space between us humming with unspoken questions.

A young server with a pierced lip and blue hair brought us menus.

"What can I get you?" the server asked, barely glancing in my direction.

Tea. I'd asked her for tea.

"Black tea with milk, please," I said after a pause longer than it should've been.

Veronica's lips curved. Her eyes danced.

"Peppermint tea," she said, voice low, like a touch along my ribs.

The server slipped away, leaving me alone with a woman who looked at me in an exhilarating and terrifying way.

"Is this... common for you?" I asked. "Making time for hapless strangers who ask for directions?"

It was an effort to sound casual, but I needed to know: was this anything special?

She laughed, warm and surprising.

"Not exactly." Her fingers traced the edge of the table—casual, precise. She knew the effect she had.

"But when I take an interest in something," she added, meeting my gaze, "I tend to follow through."

I was in trouble.

This was a woman who made me *feel* entirely, achingly, inescapably.

I should've been back at my flat with a book.

Instead, I sat across from her in a dimly lit café, watching her tuck a strand of hair behind her ear, her lips curving around her teacup.

She looked up and caught my gaze, and I felt a peculiar sensation of falling without moving at all.

I should've said something clever. Something charming.

Something to prove I wasn't just a bumbling academic who'd stumbled into her shop like a blind man fumbling for a light switch.

But I couldn't stop watching her.

Couldn't stop the wild, untamable want that surged every time she looked at me like I might be worth figuring out.

"Simon," she said, my name a teasing drawl that sent another jolt through me. "You're staring."

I flushed.

"Forgive me," I said, fumbling for an excuse. "I'm not—"

"Used to this," she finished, smiling. "I know."

She leaned in, chin resting in her hand.

And I had the distinct impression I was a puzzle she fully intended to solve.

And God help me—

I wanted to let her.

Chapter Four

VERONICA

I hadn't expected him to stay.

Not because he was rude—he wasn't. If anything, he was painfully polite.

But that kind of politeness usually came with distance.

A quiet kind of retreat.

Not this.

Not the way he looked at me now, like he didn't quite know what to do with me, but wanted to figure it out anyway.

Like he was trying to see past the polish, to the parts most people missed.

Or didn't bother looking for.

Maybe that's what caught me off guard.

Not that he was still here, but that I *wanted* him to be.

I wasn't used to this.

The quiet pull of someone watching without expectation.

Curiosity without conquest.

And something deeper woven through every glance, like he wanted to understand.

Not dissect. Not tame. Just... *understand*.

It was disarming. And dangerous. Because if I weren't careful, I might start wanting to be understood.

"If you're interested," I said lightly, not quite meeting his eyes, "there's a book club at the shop. Once a month. A little wine, a lot of opinionated women. We're discussing *Delta of Venus* next week."

He blinked. "I'm... not familiar with that one."

"Erotic short stories," I said, watching him over the rim of my cup. "Anaïs Nin. Intimate. Lyrical. Focused on female desire—and all the ways women are taught to contain it."

A flush crept up his neck.

But he didn't look away.

"I think," I added, voice soft but steady, "you'd find it... enlightening."

"I'd like that," he said quietly.

And I believed him.

**

The wine glasses were already set out. The candles lit.

I adjusted a stack of books on the display table—*Delta of Venus*, spines soft from use, pages dog-eared.

There was always a specific energy in the shop on book club nights.

A mix of anticipation and permission.

The kind of hum that builds in your chest before you let yourself say something true.

Usually I looked forward to it.

Tonight, I wasn't sure what I felt.

Simon had said he'd come.

Quietly. Simply. Like he meant it.

And for reasons I hadn't examined too closely, that possibility had been sitting under my skin all week.

I didn't *need* him to come. That wasn't the point.

But I kept imagining what it might feel like to see him walk in.

To watch him navigate a room full of women talking about longing, autonomy, sex, and power.

I smoothed a hand over the back of a chair and glanced toward the door.

I hadn't told anyone he might come.

Because I wasn't sure what it meant if he did.

But I knew one thing.

I wasn't ready to stop finding out.

The shop filled quickly—laughter and voices lacing through the low hum of music.

Women browsed, poured wine, and settled into chairs.

It was the kind of crowd that could generate more energy than a rock concert.

I watched it all from behind the counter, trying to feel like myself.

Trying to feel *anything* but the restless anticipation building all day.

And then the bell chimed.

A figure stepped through the door, shoulders a little too tight.

Simon.

He scanned the room, his eyes brushing each face, and his posture slightly hesitant, like he was bracing for impact.

Then he saw me.

And something eased.

He moved toward the counter, each step more certain.

I met him halfway, a small, unbidden smile tugging at my mouth.

"You came," I said, trying not to sound surprised.

"I did," Simon said, just a hint of uncertainty in his voice. "I hope that's... permissible."

I laughed, the sound instinctive.

"Of course it's permissible, Professor. I invited you."

He gave me a look, half sheepish, half relieved.

"Right."

He glanced around the room. "I have a feeling I'll be out of my depth."

I ran my fingers over the stack of books.

"Good."

The corners of his mouth twitched. "Good?"

"Means you might learn something."

"I'm hoping to," he said.

The weight of it landed between us.

A slight shiver swept down my spine.

And I tried, unsuccessfully, not to enjoy it.

SIMON

I hadn't meant for the words to sound quite so... loaded.

But there it was, *I'm hoping to,* hanging between us like a truth I hadn't known I'd say aloud.

Veronica didn't flinch.

She just watched me with that sharp, unreadable calm.

Like she already knew how far out of my depth I was and was letting me drown with exquisite patience.

God help me, I didn't want to leave.

I followed her through the shop as she greeted familiar faces, her presence easy and composed.

The room buzzed with a quiet energy that made my pulse kick, half nerves, half something I didn't know how to name.

She gestured to a seat in the circle of chairs near the book display, *Delta of Venus* at the center like an altar.

I sat, adjusting my posture to look less rigid than I felt.

The women were mid-conversation, laughing, arguing, riffing off one another with the kind of intimacy that made me feel like I'd stumbled into someone else's dream.

And still, not one of them blinked at my presence.

No glances. No questions. Just space. Open and deliberate.

Veronica sat beside me, crossing her legs, wine balanced easily on one knee.

I had the absurd urge to loosen my collar, even though I wasn't wearing one.

Someone made a quip about one of the stories.

I caught a phrase: *the audacity of want.*

It hit me like a strike to the ribs.

Veronica leaned in, voice pitched low. "You don't have to say anything, Professor. Just listen."

I nodded. Grateful.

And I did.

To women talking about bodies. Boundaries. Wanting without apology.

It wasn't polite.

It wasn't abstract.

It was raw.

Uncensored.

And it shook me.

I wasn't sure how long I sat there, caught in the rhythm of their voices.

But at some point, I stopped feeling like an intruder.

And started feeling like a student again.

Of literature. Of language. Of what it meant to live inside a body and own every part of it.

When Veronica looked at me, eyes warm, expression unreadable, I let myself look back.

Not just *at* her. But *into* her.

And for the first time in my life, I didn't want distance.

I wanted to stay in the heat of it.

And see what I might learn.

***

The crowd had thinned. Voices softened.

I sat quietly, empty wine glass in my hand, still reeling from what I'd just witnessed.

Not a lecture.

Not a panel.

Something else entirely.

Messy. Vital. Human.

Women speaking without softening the edges.

No apologies for wanting.

It was unsettling.

And awe-inspiring.

And Veronica, Christ, Veronica, she hadn't led so much as *held* the room.

Letting others shine.

Steering the current without ever needing to command it.

She was incandescent.

And somehow made it look effortless.

I stood as someone passed by, murmuring good night.

Veronica was near the display table, back to me, smoothing the tablecloth with distracted focus.

I crossed to her before I could lose my nerve.

"You were right," I said softly.

She glanced over her shoulder. "About what?"

I cleared my throat, hands in my pockets to avoid reaching for her.

"That I'd learn something."

A small smile tugged at her mouth, but she didn't turn.

"And?" she asked.

I exhaled. "I've spent most of my life talking about passion without the faintest clue how it actually works."

That made her turn.

Her expression unreadable.

But her eyes—God, her eyes—searched mine with quiet intensity.

"You held your own."

"I didn't say a word."

"Exactly," she said. "You listened. Most men would've tried to explain something halfway through."

"I was tempted," I admitted.

Her smile deepened.

I stepped closer.

The air shifted. Tightened.

"I felt..." I hesitated. "Unsteady. But in a good way."

"That's what growth feels like," she said.

"And desire?"

Her gaze flicked to mine, heat and something like surprise rising in her eyes.

"That," she said softly, "depends on the person."

Another beat passed. Two.

"I'd like to walk you home, if you'll permit me," I said.

Knowing it *did*.

Veronica tilted her head, studying me like a puzzle half-solved.

Then she nodded.

"I'll grab my coat."

Chapter Five

VERONICA

I turned before he could answer, slipping into the back room and pressing a hand to my chest, as if that might calm the flutter beneath it.

Stupid.

I wasn't a girl with a crush. I was a woman who knew the difference between attraction and something that could burn you alive.

And Simon Radcliffe was heat I didn't want to walk away from.

I grabbed my coat and shrugged it on slowly, giving myself a moment.

We walked in silence for a block.

It wasn't uncomfortable. Just... taut.

Quiet in the way things are right before they shift.

The click of my heels echoed faintly.

His stride matched mine, unhurried, even, though I could feel the tension beneath the surface.

Like he was afraid he'd ruin it if he moved too fast.

"You're not really used to this, are you?" I asked.

He glanced over, mouth twitching. "That obvious?"

"Only a little."

A breath passed between us.

"You make it feel like there's no wrong thing to say," he said. "Like I don't have to be anything but... this."

I looked straight ahead, pretending his words hadn't lodged somewhere dangerously close to my center.

"I don't need you to impress me, Simon."

"Then what do you need?"

It wasn't flirtation.

Just a question—honest, open, a little terrifying.

I stopped in front of my building.

The streetlight cast his features in soft shadow—eyes searching, posture just a little too proper.

What did I need?

I didn't know.

But I wanted him to be part of the answer.

"Would you like to come up for a drink?" I asked.

He hesitated and then nodded. "Yes, very much so."

I walked into my apartment and for the first time in longer than I cared to admit, I didn't feel alone in the room.

The door clicked shut, settling in my chest like a second heartbeat.

He stood just inside, taking it all in.

"May I—" he started, then caught himself. "May I look around?"

That startled a laugh from me. "It's not a museum, Professor. Make yourself at home."

He stepped in slowly, fingers brushing the edge of a bookshelf as if the books might whisper back.

I moved to the bar and poured two fingers of scotch into a pair of cut crystal tumblers.

Something warm flickered across his face as I handed him one. "Thank you."

We didn't toast.

"I think," he said, voice lower now, "your home is exactly what I expected. And nothing like I expected."

I arched a brow. "That sounds like something a man says when he's afraid of getting it wrong."

"Not afraid," he murmured. "Just... careful."

He took a sip, gaze never quite leaving mine.

"Is it working?" I asked softly.

He tilted his head. "What?"

"The carefulness."

He smiled slightly. "No."

Good.

Because I didn't want careful. Not from him. Not tonight.

I moved to the couch, curling my legs beneath me, lamplight catching the silk of my blouse.

He stood a moment longer, then followed, settling beside me with the stiff caution I was starting to find endearing.

I took a sip of scotch, letting it warm its way down.

"You always this tense around women who invite you in?"

He looked down, sheepish. "Only the ones who make me forget how to breathe."

I didn't look away. Didn't tease. Didn't pretend I didn't feel it too.

Instead, I asked, quietly, "What are you afraid will happen if you stop trying to be so proper with me?"

He swallowed.

For a long second, I thought he might deflect.

But then, voice rougher now, he said— "That I'll want more."

Then he looked at me, really looked, and I saw the truth in it.

That *wanting more* wasn't flirtation for him.

It was a risk. A leap.

And the only way he knew how to jump was with both feet.

God help me, I wanted to jump with him.

"What happens," I whispered, "if I want more too?"

The question hung between us, unguarded.

His eyes darkened.

His breath caught.

I leaned in, feeling his warmth and restraint, which made me want him more.

His hand curled behind my neck, fingers threading into my hair.

His forehead brushed mine.

And in a breath, more exhale than sound, he whispered: "Veronica, may I kiss you?"

SIMON

The words escaped before I could stop them. Polite. Measured. Ridiculously formal.

Bloody hell.

I closed my eyes, mortified. Not by the wanting, but by how I'd said it. Like I was requesting a library book. Like I didn't know how to want something without wrapping it in manners and restraint.

Why couldn't I just act? Why couldn't I reach for her?

But instead, I'd asked.

Because that's what I'd been taught, to keep desire folded beneath language. To ask instead of risk.

And now she'd laugh. Or tell me I was sweet, but—

"Yes."

A single, steady word.

My eyes snapped open.

She wasn't teasing. She meant it.

Every nerve surged toward her, toward this moment I'd nearly ruined by trying too hard to do it right.

I didn't ask again.

I leaned in, slow, deliberate, hand skimming her jaw. Her breath hitched. Her lips parted.

And I kissed her.

Not tentative. Not timid.

Not anymore.

It was nothing like I'd imagined. It was everything. Her mouth, soft and urgent beneath mine, lit me up like a live wire. Wild. Unrestrained. Like she was daring me to want her more, and I did.

Her fingers curled into my hair, pulling me closer, and I was lost. Hopelessly, gloriously lost.

She shifted into my lap, making a slight sound at contact that nearly undid me.

Everything I'd kept locked tightly shook loose, no manners or control. Just heat and the feel of her moving against me like she'd been waiting for this too.

She pulled back, just slightly. I felt the loss like a physical ache. But then her mouth was at my ear, her breath warm.

"Simon..."

A low groan escaped me, and she smiled against my skin, a victorious thing that sent my heart slamming.

Her lips brushed my jaw, the corner of my mouth—

Then kissed me again. Slow. Deep. A decadent promise.

My fingers clenched against her hip, pulling her into me. Every instinct screamed to slow down. Rein it in. But I didn't. I couldn't. I just kept falling. And she kept catching me.

Her fingers found the buttons of my shirt, deft and sure. A laugh caught in my throat, turned to a groan as her mouth followed the path she'd laid bare, down my neck, across my collarbone.

I couldn't think. Couldn't breathe. Didn't care.

I'd spent my life terrified of slipping.

Now it felt like the only thing that made sense.

I wanted to tell her that.

Tell her everything.

But even if I'd had the words, I wouldn't have said them. Not with her hands on my chest, her hips rocking against mine, her mouth hot and demanding.

She moved lower, and my entire body arched.

Her fingers were at my belt, working it loose, breath hot against my stomach.

The button of my trousers slid open.

My heart pounded, wild and unrelenting.

Her hand slipped past the waistband of my boxers—

And I gasped. Actually gasped, like a schoolboy, as her fingers closed around me.

"Christ," I breathed, my head tipping back against the couch as she pulled me free.

And her mouth moved lower, and, God, lower still.

Chapter Six

SIMON

Her breath trailed over me like a warm breeze, exhaling a trembling caress that set my nerves humming. When her lips hovered just above my skin, I felt every molecule of air sizzle against me. My chest rose and fell in quick, shallow beats, my heart a trapped bird.

I was undone and I didn't mind. I'd never felt so exquisitely alive.

She pressed her mouth to me at last. A feather-light kiss. Then a gentle suck that sent fire rippling through my veins.

I gasped, arching instinctively, chasing the pleasure down.

Her tongue slid out, warm, deliberate, painting me with slow strokes that left me shaking. Each flick teased a fresh jolt of heat, slick friction building in ways I could barely process.

My hands tangled in her hair, anchoring her to me. She smiled against my skin, then deepened her focus, lips parting, tongue tracing bold, devastating patterns.

My breathing turned ragged. Sounds I couldn't contain spilled out.

My hips lifted of their own accord, seeking her, needing her, drawn by something primal.

"Veronica—" Her name broke from me in a whisper, more plea than word.

The world narrowed to where her mouth met me, where nothing else existed. She worked me over with fierce, tender precision, like she lived solely to bring me to this edge.

Waves crashed through me, each one higher, sharper, until I was weightless.

Then, impossibly, I went over.

The center of me collapsed into a pinpoint of pleasure. Muscles clenched. Breath caught. For a moment, the edges of my vision blurred.

I cried out her name, again and again, a single soaring note echoing in my skull.

Even as my body shook, she held me there, unrelenting, devoted, until I was spent and shivering, awash in the warm afterglow.

She rose slowly, spine curving with impossible grace.

Her hair tumbled around her shoulders, glossy waves framing her face.

She settled back onto my lap and our eyes met.

My pulse thundered in my ears.

"I didn't mean to ruin you this soon," she murmured, voice low and playful.

"You haven't ruined me," I whispered, breathless. My hands slid to her hips, fingers pressing into her. "Veronica," I said, soft with longing, "will you teach me?"

She paused.

That question hung between us like a dare.

"Teach you?" she echoed, tasting the word. Desire coiled in my belly.

I swallowed. "How to give you this," I said, gesturing to the charged space still thrumming between us. "How to make you feel what you've made me feel. I want to learn everything you like, everything you crave."

"Everything?" she murmured, breath warm against my lips. "You sure you're ready for that?"

My chest rose in a fierce inhale. "I've never been more sure of anything," I said, all of me alight with certainty.

VERONICA

I had never wanted to teach. Never longed to guide a man's hands, his lips, his movements, until Simon.

The thought of revealing every contour of my desire to him sent a shiver racing down my spine, a delicious tremor that felt as forbidden as it was inevitable.

"Consider it extra credit," I murmured, leaning in until our chests touched. My thumb traced his bottom lip—soft, yielding—and I swallowed hard against the pulse hammering in my throat.

No one had unraveled me like this. I'd never allowed myself to *need* someone so completely. But Simon...

God, I wanted him.

His gaze held mine steady, unwavering.

"Tell me what to do," he whispered, voice rough with anticipation.

My fingertips hovered at the hem of my blouse, silk cool under my nails.

"Unbutton my blouse," I breathed. "And unhook my bra."

His fingers brushed the nape of my neck—a teasing graze—then dropped to the first button.

He freed it slowly, fabric slipping against skin, a trail of fire in its wake.

I arched into him, craving the friction.

His pupils were wide, luminous in the lamplight. He eased the last button open, and the blouse slid from my shoulders.

Ivory lace framed my breasts, delicate against bare skin.

I'd never let a man undress me like this, *savoring* every moment.

Simon nudged the straps down my arms, then unclasped my bra.

Cool air kissed my chest, and I shivered, aching.

"Simon," I whispered. "Suck on my nipples. Pinch them. I want to feel your mouth."

He paused—then obeyed.

His lips closed over my right nipple, warm and wet, and a rush of heat blossomed through me.

His tongue moved in slow, maddening spirals. I gasped, fingers curling into his hair

His other hand found my left breast, fingers pinching, twisting.

I couldn't think—only *feel*: the heat of his mouth, the scrape of stubble.

I let my head fall back, hips grinding on his lap.

He groaned—a low, hungry sound that sent a rush of wetness to my pussy.

I tangled my fingers in his hair, holding him there, unwilling to let go.

He moved to my right breast again, coaxing another moan from me.

"Lower, Simon," I gasped. "I need your mouth lower."

He lifted his head. Lamplight caught the sweat at his temple, his pupils like smoldering coals.

"Tell me," he rasped. "What do you want?"

I stood, my fingers fumbled at the waistband of my pants.

I slid them down, panties with them—bare in seconds.

Cool air kissed my thighs, and heat bloomed between them.

He leaned in, nostrils flaring, as if he could smell my need.

"Use your tongue," I said, voice shaking.

"On my clit—curl around it, suck it, swirl it."

The words lit him up.

His hands gripped my hips, shifting me to sit on the edge of the couch, his thumbs grazing bare skin as he lowered himself between my legs.

My breath caught.

First—a flick. Soft. Teasing.

Then the broad sweep of his tongue over my clit.

I gasped, my hips jerking at the contact.

Each flick a spark, each swirl a wave, building into something sharp and inevitable.

Chapter Seven

VERONICA

He closed his lips around me, warm and slick, and a low, guttural groan vibrated straight through my pelvis. He moved with deliberate pressure, sucking until my knees threatened to buckle. I clutched his hair, tugging him closer, caught between the sting of need and the exquisite burn behind my eyes.

"I need your fingers, too," I gasped, voice raw. "Inside me—while you use your mouth."

He paused, breath hitching—then I felt two strong fingers press against my entrance. He curled them upward, pushing them into my wet heat. I arched against him, hips rocking on instinct.

"Christ, you're wet," he growled. "Sweet and tangy—so fucking good."

The words hit like sparks. He added a third finger, stretching me, while his mouth found my clit again, moving in time with his fingers. I was drowning—slick pulses, suction, the slide of flesh against flesh. My nails scraped down his scalp as I chased the pleasure higher.

"Like this?" he asked, breathless, fingers speeding up, angle sharper.

"Yes," I choked out. "Oh God, yes."

I trembled on the brink, world reduced to the press of his fingers, the roar of blood in my ears. He was merciless, relentless.

"God, Simon." His name tumbled from my lips like prayer and demand. "Faster. Harder."

He delivered both. His fingers plunged deep, mouth unyielding, rhythm unbroken. I was all sensation, blurred vision, caught breath, and that raw, insatiable ache.

"Simon," I gasped. "You're going to make me—"

The words shattered into a cry as I came, crashing through wave after wave of release. He held steady, giving me every last stroke, until the final tremor rolled through me and I sat trembling before him.

Then he eased back, mouth trailing kisses up my body—my abdomen, ribs, throat—until he hovered over me, eyes dark and gleaming.

I was still panting, stunned by how fully I'd let go.

"Did I..." He hesitated, tousled, and flushed. "Was that...?"

"Perfect," I said, laughing softly at the wonder in his voice. "God, Simon. It was perfect."

Beneath that word was a thousand others—unreal, overwhelming, *more*.

He kissed me, deep and unhurried, and I tasted myself on his lips.

It stole my breath. My fingers clenched on his shoulders, gripping like I didn't want him to leave my body or orbit.

"Veronica," he murmured. The way he said my name—thick with need—reignited everything.

He lowered himself against me, and I felt his cock: solid, insistent, that low ache of wanting more already surging again.

"Veronica..." he said, voice unsteady. "I want to. God, I want to. I just—"

He paused, frustration catching.

"I don't know if I'll be any good at it..."

The admission landed between us.

I smiled, slow and sure, and reached for him. His shoulders eased.

"You will," I said, voice rough with want. "Trust me. You're better at this than you think."

I rolled my hips against his, and this time he didn't hesitate.

He reached between us, tore open a condom with shaking fingers, and rolled it on. Then he thrust into me—deep and urgent and so fucking good I cried out. The angle. The pressure. He drove into me like he meant to claim every part of me.

I wrapped my legs around him, opening fully, taking all of him. His forehead dropped to my shoulder. I felt his tension—his restraint—and I wanted to shatter it.

I rolled my hips, caught his breath with my own, and I *felt* it—

The shift.

He stopped holding back.

"Veronica—" he groaned, ragged and raw. A plea. A promise. A man unraveling.

I met him at every thrust, my body winding tighter with each stroke.

His mouth found mine, frantic, consuming, and I drank him in—his wildness, his hunger, the way he gave himself without condition.

I didn't know when I'd last felt this alive.

SIMON

Her body gripped me—wet, hot, perfect—and I nearly lost it right then.

It was too much and not enough, and all I could do was move—slow at first, then faster, chasing the rising heat. She met every thrust with a flex of her hips, a breathless sound that undid me completely.

I'd never felt anything like this. Never *let* myself.

But here I was, inside her, part of her, and I didn't want to stop.

Didn't want to be careful. Didn't want control.

I just wanted *this*.

I thrust harder, deeper, chasing the wild, exquisite breaking point I'd been skirting since the moment I stepped through her door.

The sounds from my throat were foreign, raw, and ragged. The heat of her, the sheer, glorious heat of her, pulled everything from me.

"God, Veronica—" My voice cracked. "I want to make sure you—"

She knew. Of course she knew.

She rocked against me, her hand slipping between us, rubbing her clit in tight, relentless circles. The sight—her fingers, her abandon—blurred my vision.

"Christ, yes," I groaned. "God, yes, Veronica—"

It was the sexiest thing I'd ever seen.

Her body arched, pressing against me as I fucked her—hard, hungry, out of control.

And I felt it: the tightening, the pulse, the wild rhythm of her release building beneath me.

I was going to die.

And I didn't care.

She cried out my name, and I was right there with her.

The world went white.

I came hard, hips jerking, everything blurring into heat and light and the feel of her clenching around me. There was no end, no edge—just her and me, together, completely.

We collapsed in a tangle of limbs and ragged breath, her skin damp beneath mine, and I didn't want to leave it. Didn't want to leave *her*.

I rolled to the side, drawing her with me. She exhaled a long, contented sigh. I wanted to stay like this. Wake up like this.

Want her like this—and not be afraid of it.

"Jesus, Simon," she said, breathless and unguarded. "Where the hell did that come from?"

I smiled against her hair. "You," I said simply. "All you."

She hummed low in her throat, curling into me. Closer than I'd let anyone get in years.

We didn't speak. We didn't have to.

The silence wrapped around us, warm and full.

I watched her settle. I saw her smile. And I wanted more, more than a night, more than a flicker of something impossible.

I was still reeling. From the way she'd let me in. From the way she'd made me feel like someone *new*. I wanted to say something, *anything*, to show her what she'd done to me. For me.

But the words tangled.

"Veronica..." I paused, heat rising in my cheeks. "That was... I mean... God. Thank you."

She stilled. Her body tensed against mine. "Thank you?"

Shit.

"I mean—for this. For... everything. I've never—" I stopped. Breathed. "I've never let myself feel like this. I didn't know..."

The silence stretched and then slowly the tension in her body dissolved.

"You make it sound like a favor," she said, voice dry. "Like I'm running a charity for repressed academics."

A shaky laugh escaped me. "If you are, it's remarkably effective."

Her mouth twitched, lips brushing my throat. "Good. Because I don't plan on stopping."

Another laugh, real and low, tumbled out of me. "Is that so?"

"Mmmm," she said, smug and unapologetic. "Think you can handle it?"

I thought about life before her. Before *this*.

All the days I'd let pass, restless and half-lived.

"I'd like to try."

She made a satisfied sound, her hand sliding up to rest over my heart.

My entire life, I'd lived by the rules.

But now?

I wanted to break them all.

And I wanted her to show me how.

Chapter Eight

VERONICA

My head rested on Simon's chest, and the steady beat of his heart was a reminder that this was real. That *he* was real. His fingers trailed absently along my spine, leaving a wake of warmth that made me want to roll over him and start again.

My blouse was a crumpled heap on the floor. My hair? A small electrical storm.

We were a mess. A beautiful, tangled, delicious mess.

"We should clean up," I murmured, feeling his pulse thrum beneath my cheek.

His hand stilled. "You mean...?"

I propped myself on one elbow, letting the suggestion linger.

"Shower," I said slowly. "Together."

The flush that rose up his neck was almost as satisfying as the orgasm he'd just given me.

"Right," he said, barely breathing. "Together."

I stood and stretched deliberately and tugged him to his feet. He followed, still looking adorably bewildered, like he couldn't quite believe this was happening.

In the bathroom, anticipation zinged through me. He paused at the doorway, hesitation flickering across his face.

"You'll like it," I said, voice low. "Promise."

He huffed a laugh. "I think I'll like anything you have in mind."

"Good," I said, pulling him in. "Then stop overthinking and just... enjoy."

I turned on the water and stepped beneath the spray. When he joined me, his sharp inhalation was almost enough to make me forget my name.

He reached for me, tentative but eager. I smiled, twining my arms around his neck and rising onto my toes.

"What?" I teased. "Never showered with a woman before?"

He blinked through the water. "No," he said, swallowing. "No, I haven't."

I kissed him, wet, hot, breathless, and felt him respond to me, shedding uncertainty like a too-tight skin.

His hands slid over me, smoothing under the stream like polished stone. He was learning me, each curve, each shiver, his touch growing more confident with every pass. God, he was a quick study.

I turned, water sluicing down my spine. When I pressed back against his chest, I felt the firm line of his arousal nestled in the hollow of my ass.

I rocked, slow and deliberate—wet skin against wet skin—and he gasped, fingers digging into my hips to hold me steady.

His hands swept over my sides—slick, greedy. I tilted my head back, heat pulsing through me, until I trembled at the seams.

"Veronica..." he whispered, reverent and undone. "God, Veronica."

He pulled me closer, his body moving with mine in a relentless, hungry rhythm.

"Tell me what you want," he breathed.

"Bite me," I said, voice ragged. I tilted my head, exposing that tender curve where my neck meets my shoulder.

He paused—then his teeth brushed my skin, a featherlight nip that made me gasp.

"Harder," I said.

His bite deepened—sharp, sweet, perfect—and I cried out, sensation blooming hot across my skin.

My knees buckled. I clutched his hair, the water crashing over us, the heat pooling in my pussy.

"Fuck," I gasped. "Simon, I need you."

My breath came in quick, shallow bursts. "I need you to fuck me."

He stilled.

"We don't have a condom in here," he murmured, regret heavy in his voice.

I shivered at the confessional hush.

"Then touch me," I whispered. "Here."

I guided his fingers to the slick heat of my pussy.

He didn't hesitate. I arched back, one hand on my breast, rolling my nipple between damp fingers. The other hand tangled in his hair, anchoring him to me.

He rocked against me, cock hard against my ass, mouth hot against my neck.

"Fuck, Simon—yes."

He tightened his hold, his mouth relentless.

"God, I'm close," I gasped, hips thrusting against his hand.

"Christ, Veronica—"

His cock slid between my ass cheeks, his fingers working harder as I moved against him in a desperate, perfect rhythm.

SIMON

I felt Veronica arch against me, slick and warm, wrapping around me like silk, igniting every nerve with the urge to give her more—*everything*.

I slid two fingers inside, felt her clench around me like a velvet vise. A soft gasp slipped from her lips, brushing my ear, and my thumb circled her clit, coaxing out breathless cries that sent heat roaring through my chest.

Her hips rocked, her head falling back, hair brushing my cheek.

The sounds I made were unrecognizable—low, rough groans echoing off the tile.

"Simon," she breathed. "God, Simon—"

Her body tightened, a perfect bowstring drawn to breaking. And then she came, shuddering, my name spilling from her in a cracked, beautiful cry. Her pleasure pulsed around me, holding me there, and I came undone with her—wild, searing, everything at once.

"Jesus," I managed, voice low with awe. "I didn't know it was possible to feel like that."

Veronica turned, flushed and radiant. I kissed her, slow and lingering, tasting the last edge of what we'd shared.

We stood tangled beneath the cooling water until she murmured, "Come on. Before we turn into prunes."

I followed her out, legs trembling, heart still racing. She tossed me a towel, and I watched, mesmerized, as she dried off with the kind of languid grace that undid me completely.

She caught my gaze and smiled, unguarded and stunning. I held my breath. But then she laced her fingers through mine and tugged me toward the bedroom.

The bed was a tangle of sheets and temptation. She shoved me onto it, crawling after me with a feline grace that stole every coherent thought. She settled against me, head on my chest, her leg draped possessively over mine.

"Veronica," I said before I could stop myself. "This isn't just—"

"A fling?" she said, warm, teasing. "An experiment? A phase?"

My stomach clenched. "I didn't mean—"

"Relax, Professor." She nuzzled my chest. "I know it's not."

I exhaled. "It's not," I said, voice low. "Not for me."

She shifted, sliding over me in a way that made my pulse stutter.

"Good," she murmured. "Because it isn't for me either."

Relief washed through me, bone-deep. I hadn't realized how much I needed to hear it. That she meant it.

Her cheek rested against my chest, her breath syncing with mine. I let my hand drift through her damp hair and fell asleep unguarded for the first time in my life.

I woke once, dreams slipping away like smoke. She was still curled beside me, her breath steady. I pulled her close and let her warmth lull me back under.

The second time I woke, the room was painted in the blue hush of early morning. Her leg still draped over mine, her head tucked into my shoulder. My heart surged with something wild and tender.

Her hair spilled like silk across my chest. I didn't want to move.

But then my phone rang.

Bloody hell.

I should have ignored it. Let it go to voicemail.

But that old, tidy part of me, the one that never missed meetings, won.

I slipped out of bed, careful not to wake her. She murmured something and turned onto her stomach, the sheets tangling around her like an invitation.

My trousers were in a heap in the living room. I dug out the phone.

Miranda.

Of course.

She always had a knack for calling at the worst possible moment.

I hesitated. My thumb hovered.

But I answered.

"Hello?" I said softly, stepping further from the bedroom.

"Simon," Miranda said, her voice crisp. "Did I catch you at a bad time?"

Chapter Nine

VERONICA

The first thing I registered was the warmth beside me was gone.

The second was his voice.

Low. Measured.

Not the sleep-rough murmur I'd fallen asleep to, but something sharper. Controlled.

I blinked against the pale morning light. The sheets were cool where his body had been. The air still smelled like him, musk and soap and something wild from the night before.

I sat up slowly, the sheet slipping down, as his voice filtered in from the other room.

Not angry.

Not intimate.

But... familiar.

"Miranda," he said, the name cutting clean through the quiet. "You are my ex-wife. *Ex*-wife. That doesn't give you the right to keep tabs on me."

My chest tightened. Ex-wife. I had no idea. He hadn't mentioned her. Not once.

Was this why he was so cautious? Was I a rebound—something reckless to shake off routine?

Then I heard him say: "No, I'm not seeing anyone. Though that's really none of your business, is it?"

The words landed like a slap. Not seeing anyone. Maybe it shouldn't have meant so much. It had only been a handful of days. One passion filled night. But it had felt like more. Like something real. Something I wasn't ready to lose.

I wasn't supposed to care. But I did. Because last night, he hadn't touched me like I was temporary. He'd touched me like I *mattered*.

Maybe it was innocent. Maybe it was complicated. But he hadn't told me about her. And now—whatever we were—was already starting to fray.

I stepped back from the door. Quiet. Careful.

Because suddenly, I didn't know where I stood.

***

I was fully dressed by the time he stepped into the room.

He wore only his boxers—hair tousled, chest bare, still soft from sleep.

And he looked... hopeful.

Like nothing had changed.

Like he didn't know I'd heard him.

Didn't know I'd woken to the sound of my name being erased—swept aside with a polite *No, I'm not seeing anyone.*

Like the night we'd shared hadn't happened.

Like I hadn't let him in.

And yes, it had only been a few days.

But I hadn't imagined what was building between us.

"You're up," he said, surprised. His smile faltered as took in the fact that I was fully dressed.

"I was hoping to crawl back in bed with you."

I forced a smile. It didn't reach anything inside me.

"Sorry," I said lightly. "I need to get to the shop. Early shipment."

"Oh. I—of course."

His eyes dropped to his bare legs. "My clothes are..."

"In the living room," I said. "I'll wait."

He hesitated, like he wanted to ask something, but turned away instead.

I listened to the rustle of clothes, the zip of trousers, the thud of shoes. When I was certain he was dressed, I went into the living room,

"Veronica, is everything—?"

"Fine," I said, too fast, walking across the room.

To avoid the silence, I opened my front door.

He stepped through slowly, still looking at me like he didn't understand what he'd done.

But he didn't press.

And I didn't explain.

The door clicked shut behind him.

Only then did I let myself sag against it, breath tight, questions sharp beneath my ribs.

SIMON

The door clicked shut behind me—soft, but final.

Like something had ended, and I hadn't moved fast enough to stop it.

I raked a hand through my hair, heart pounding beneath the weight of my own words.

No, I'm not seeing anyone.

Christ.

I hadn't meant it like that. Not for her. Not for *us*.

Miranda didn't deserve the truth. She never had. She collected secrets like currency. Spent them without care. I'd learned to keep things close.

Too close.

But Veronica had heard me.

I saw it in her eyes—calm where there used to be a spark. Guarded where there'd been light.

She hadn't said a word.

She hadn't needed to.

The shift was surgical.

And God, I didn't want to lose her.

Not like this.

Not over a sentence I didn't mean.

I leaned against the wall, trying to breathe past the hollow thrum in my chest.

She made me feel... alive.

Like I had skin again. Like I was allowed to want. To be wanted.

And now she was pulling away.

I didn't blame her.

But I couldn't accept it either.

Her name was still stuck in my throat.

I stepped outside, the cool morning air biting my neck.

I didn't know what this was.

What to call it.

But I knew one thing: I wasn't ready for it to end.

Not like this.

The walk to the café was a blur. A loop of things I *should* have said. The same server with blue hair took my order.

"Tea," I said. "Black."

I sat in the corner, away from the bustle, and waited.

For what, I wasn't sure.

Time to pass.

My heart to fall back in line.

But all I saw was how she looked this morning, like I was already a memory.

I couldn't let that happen.

She deserved more than silence. More than a man who hadn't trusted her with the truth because someone else had twisted it.

I had to make her see that.

I had to make her *see me*.

But would she hear it if I showed up now with a fumbling explanation?

Or would she only hear the man who said *he wasn't seeing anyone*?

The server dropped the tea with a sharp clink.

I stared at it, watched the steam curl upward and vanish into nothing.

What would I even say?

That I panicked?

That I defaulted to the tidy version of myself because Miranda weaponizes vulnerability?

That I said the wrong thing to protect something that mattered more?

No. That would sound like an excuse.

And Veronica deserved *truth*.

I wasn't sure I knew how to give it.

But I had to try.

I pulled out my phone. Hovered over her name.

Don't text.

She'd see right through it. Too easy to hide behind. Too easy to misread.

If this was going to be salvaged, if *we* were going to be salvaged, I had to show up. Not as the professor. Not as the man afraid of wanting too much.

But as myself.

Flawed. Unpolished. Wanting her.

I stood and stepped back into the morning—into the ache of what I'd broken, and the one chance I had to make it right.

Chapter Ten

VERONICA

I locked the door behind him.

Then crossed the room and picked up my phone.

Vivian answered on the second ring.

"If this call doesn't involve a fashion emergency, a secret affair, or international espionage, I'm hanging up and blaming you for my under-eye circles."

"Does possibly ruining an almost-relationship with a hot Englishman count as international espionage? Because it feels dramatic enough."

I exhaled, sinking onto the couch. "Simon was married."

"And... he didn't tell you?" Vivian asked quietly.

"No," I said. "I heard him on the phone. I woke up to it. Her name is Miranda. His ex-wife."

"Yikes," she said. Then, after a pause: "Okay. That's not great. But it's also not... catastrophic."

"He never mentioned her. Not once."

"Did you ask?"

The question landed with a thud.

"What?"

"Did you ask if he'd ever been married? Or were you waiting for him to volunteer it?"

I opened my mouth.

Closed it.

"No," I admitted.

Vivian made a sleepy noise. "Okay, so... he didn't lie. He just didn't hand over the whole syllabus on day three."

I sighed. "It wasn't just that."

"Of course not. There's more."

I swallowed. "He told her he wasn't seeing anyone."

"Well. Shit," Vivian said, not even trying to soften it.

"Yeah."

"Did he say it like... 'I'm not seeing anyone because I'm actually not' or like 'please stop asking me personal questions you nosy harpy'?"

"It sounded... clipped. Like he didn't want her to know."

"Okay, well, ex-wives are exes for a reason. Maybe he didn't want to give her ammunition."

"Or maybe I was a curiosity. Something not worth mentioning."

"Stop. You don't believe that."

I didn't answer.

Vivian sighed. "Ver. You let a man into your bed. You don't do that lightly. And I don't think he took it lightly either."

"I don't know what I'm doing."

"You're protecting yourself. I get it. But maybe—just maybe—don't write him off for one badly timed phone call."

"I didn't write him off."

"You threw him out like he was trying to recruit you for a cult."

"Viv."

She softened. "Just don't let fear do all the talking, okay?"

I exhaled again, softer this time. "Okay. Thanks."

We hung up.

And the silence settled in, thick and humming like it always did when something important had just shifted.

I stared at the ceiling.

What was I doing?

Last night hadn't just been sex. It had been... *more*. The way he'd touched me. The way he'd held me afterward. The way he'd looked at me like I was a revelation, not a risk.

He'd made me feel *seen*. Not just the polished parts. The quiet, messy ones. The ones who never felt safe with someone else in the room.

And he hadn't treated them like burdens.

I pressed my fingers to my lips, remembering the press of his mouth—hesitant, reverent, hungry. That soft gasp when I kissed his throat. The ache. The sweetness.

He'd touched me like he couldn't believe he was allowed to.

And I'd let him in. Not just to my bed.

To *everything*.

Maybe that's what scared me most.

I stood, pacing to the window, watching the sun stretch across the street like it didn't know anything had changed.

Maybe it hadn't.

Maybe I'd panicked.

He hadn't lied. I hadn't asked. And when Miranda called, he sounded like a man doing damage control, not erasing me.

I rubbed the back of my neck, jaw tight.

Vivian was right.

I was protecting myself.

But maybe I was also pushing away the one thing that had ever felt worth keeping.

I didn't know what came next.

But I knew I owed him more than silence.

SIMON

The shop window glowed warm against the dusky street, casting shadows like a stage before curtain rise.

I paused just outside the door, heart pounding far too loudly for a man who'd once lectured in front of a hundred first-years with coffee on his tie and barely a note to guide him.

This was different.

This was *her*.

The bell chimed as I stepped inside. The air was warm, faintly perfumed—amber, spice, something floral I couldn't name but would know for the rest of my life.

She was behind the counter, reaching for her keys.

She looked up.

Paused.

Didn't say a word.

I cleared my throat. "Pardon me," I said, tugging at my sleeve like it might save me. "I was wondering if you could help me find something."

She watched me, one brow arched.

"For a woman," I added. "She's... remarkable. In an exquisite, devastating sort of way. Brilliant. Self-possessed. The kind who makes a man forget how doors work. Or speech."

Still nothing. But the corner of her mouth twitched—just slightly.

"She runs a shop like this, actually. The kind that makes a buttoned-up Brit immediately regret his life choices. And yet... makes him want to be brave."

That earned me a look. Sharp. Curious. And something else—something just shy of fond.

"So," I said, lightly resting my hand on the display case, "what do you recommend for someone like her?"

Veronica tilted her head, lips curving into what might've been forgiveness—or a challenge.

She stepped around the counter, slow and deliberate.

"I suppose that depends," she said. "What are you hoping to give her?"

I met her eyes. Let the mask drop.

"Something honest," I said. "Something that says I'm still here. Still hoping. Still serious."

She didn't answer right away.

She just looked at me, quiet and unreadable, as if still deciding what part of herself to show.

Then she turned, her fingers skimming a display shelf. She selected a small black box—discreet and elegant—and placed it gently on the counter.

"This one," she said. "Elegant. Focused. Builds slowly, but steadily. No shortcuts."

Her voice was even, but something softer flickered underneath.

She tapped the top of the box once. "It's my favorite. Not because it's the strongest, but because it knows what it's doing. No pretending. No performance. Just... consistent, honest pressure. Until you can't ignore it anymore."

My breath caught.

She wasn't just handing me a toy.

She was handing me the truth—hers, mine, maybe ours.

I stepped closer.

"So I gather you heard the phone call this morning," I said quietly.

Something flickered in her eyes.

"I didn't tell you about Miranda," I went on, "not because I meant to lie—but because I liked what we were building too much to let her contaminate it. I didn't want her name anywhere near *this*."

She didn't speak.

I swallowed. "And when I said I wasn't seeing any-one—it wasn't about you. It was about her. Miranda twists things. Always has. She turns details into weapons. I've spent years keeping my life from becoming her ammu-nition."

I looked down.

Then back up.

"But you're not a secret. You're the most *real* thing I've felt in a long time. And I should've said that. I should've said everything."

The silence between us deepened. Not cold—just full.

I didn't reach for her.

Didn't press.

I just stood there.

Hopeful.

Chapter Eleven

VERONICA

I stared at him.

At this man who once couldn't get through a sentence without blushing, now standing in my shop, spine straight, eyes clear, laying himself bare.

No excuses. No deflection.

Just truth.

And that made it harder.

It would've been so much easier to be angry, to cut him off clean, file him under *mistake*, and move on.

I knew how to do that. I was good at it.

But Simon hadn't given me something easy to walk away from.

He'd given me honesty. Quiet, unpolished, terrifying honesty.

And I didn't know what to do with it.

I let the silence stretch—not to punish him, but because I needed to breathe through the ache in my chest.

The ache that came from *wanting* to believe him.

From being scared that maybe I did.

"I don't do casual," I said. "Not with people I wake up next to."

His jaw tensed. He nodded.

"And I don't do *maybes*," I added. "If this is a phase—or a rebellion—or something you'll regret when it gets messy—I need to know."

His breath hitched. "It's not."

I hesitated. "Because this morning? It sounded like I was... convenient. Temporary."

"You're not," he said, voice raw. "God, Veronica, you're not."

"But you didn't tell me about her." My voice cracked. "You didn't think I should know? Before I let you in?"

His face went pale. "I should've. I know that now."

"And then you said you weren't seeing anyone," I pressed. "Like it was true."

"I said it to keep Miranda from twisting something that wasn't hers. She turns details into spectacle. I didn't want that for you. But I know what it sounded like. And I'm sorry."

I looked at him.

Really looked.

He wasn't just sorry.

He was scared.

Because he'd felt it too—whatever this was. And he knew he'd hurt it. Hurt *me*.

And maybe this was where I told him it wasn't enough.

That I didn't trust him.

But the truth?

I did.

Maybe not entirely. Not yet.

But the idea of never seeing him again?

That hurt more than all of it combined.

I took a long breath.

"I'm still angry," I said quietly. "Still not sure what happens next."

"I don't need sure," he said. "Just... a chance."

A pause.

Then I nodded. Once.

His exhale was soft, relieved, and wrecked and reverent.

I picked up the box between us and returned it to the shelf.

Then reached for his hand.

Warm. Slightly trembling.

I didn't let go.

"I'd love to buy you a tea," I said, echoing the words he once fumbled so sweetly.

His breath caught.

And then that quiet, crooked smile flickered into place.

"I thought you'd never ask."

SIMON

The café was quiet.

Veronica sat across from me, hands wrapped around a delicate china cup. She wasn't smiling, not quite. But the edge of her mouth curved slightly when I looked at her, and for now, that was enough.

God, she was striking. Always had been. But tonight, she looked... grounded. Not soft. Not small. Just certain. Like she'd chosen to be here, fully, honestly, and somehow made space for me to do the same.

I didn't take it lightly.

"I don't know what this is," I said. "But I know I want it."

She didn't speak. Didn't rush the moment.

So I went on.

"I spent so long avoiding anything that looked like passion. Desire. Vulnerability. And then you walked in—or I did, technically—and everything I'd kept quiet cracked open."

Her gaze softened. Just slightly.

"I don't want to return to who I was before," I said. "Not after this. Not after you."

Still, she didn't answer. Just watched me—calm, steady.

And somehow, the silence didn't scare me.

It felt like trust.

Or hope.

I used to think intimacy was something you earned by being agreeable. By being easy.

But she didn't want easy.

She wanted truth.

And impossibly, I was starting to believe I could give her that.

"I'm not great at trusting what I can't control," she said.

I reached for her hand, threading my fingers through hers.

She let me hold on to her. Let me feel the warmth of her skin.

"But I'm trying."

I nodded, feeling something crack open inside me again. Something that made me want to laugh and cry and kiss her all at once.

"Good," I said, and my voice came out rougher than I intended. "Me too."

She didn't pull away. Didn't erect any walls. Her eyes stayed on mine, bright and alive and full of something I didn't dare name, even though I felt it echoing in my own chest. Her hand squeezed back, gentle at first, then firmer, a reassurance, a promise, an understanding.

We sat, linked across the table, the silence wrapping us together in a cocoon of possibility. It was as if the world outside had dimmed, leaving only us and the small, flickering candlelight that played over her face. The café turned into an intimate bubble, the clinking of silverware and muffled conversations transforming into a soft soundtrack for this tentative, newfound us.

"I'm not afraid," she said, her voice a delicious, vibrant whisper that cut through the night.

And neither was I.

Epilogue

VERONICA

It had been six months since he walked into my shop and described a woman he didn't know how to stop wanting. Six months since I'd returned the favor—every gift a new layer of trust, every unwrapping a fresh thrill.

Tonight's surprise lay snug at the base of his cock: a smooth black silicone ring, its inner rim lined with ridges and twin bullet vibrators. The moment I flicked it on, a low hum pulsed against him, steady and deliberate, like the beat of my own arousal.

His eyes widened behind his glasses, like he still couldn't believe he was allowed to want like this.

He swallowed hard, chest rising.

I curled my fingers around him, just above the ring. His cock was already slick with pre-cum, and the vibration buzzed through my palm, up my arm, straight into my core.

"Christ, Veronica," he rasped, voice trembling. "I'm not—"

"You will," I whispered, shifting to straddle him. I guided him inside, inch by inch, my nails grazing the tops of his thighs in half-moon arcs.

I sank down harder, palms braced against his knees. The ring pressed flush to my clit, every vibration a rolling drumbeat I felt in my spine.

He bucked beneath me—brief, broken thrusts that deepened the pulse between us. His hands tangled in my hair, and a jolt of tenderness raced down my spine when he gripped tight.

"You're going to make me—" he choked, words swallowed by sensation.

"Not yet," I breathed.

I held him still, watching the tension coil in his jaw, the heat rise in his cheeks, then rode him hard, fast, the vibration roaring in our blood.

His head tipped back, glasses askew, want gleaming in every line of his face. I kissed him, fierce and deep. He broke apart beneath my mouth, fingers clutching at my hips.

"Fuck," he whispered, a confession and a prayer.

I felt him tremble, whole body taut, and ground down against him, chasing my own crest as he came. The ring hummed between us, guiding me over the edge, until I shattered—loud, breathless, undone.

He pulled me close, arms tight around me as he pulsed inside me, every last wave of sensation wringing us out until there was nothing left but skin and sweat and the sweet, dizzy quiet of after.

I stayed right where I was—still straddling him, breath slowing, flushed and wrecked.

Not from the toy.

From him.

From us.

His hands rested on my hips like he wasn't ready to let go—and God, I wasn't either.

"Professor Radcliffe," I whispered, grinning. "I think you just passed the final exam."

His hand skimmed my spine, the smile he gave me half-ruined and wholly mine.

"I had an excellent teacher," he murmured.

Still catching his breath, he adjusted his glasses. "Any chance of extra credit?"

A low, sated laugh escaped me. I let my head fall back. "Always pushing for perfection," I teased, rolling my hips just enough to make him gasp.

My body still hummed with aftershocks, warmed by the slow burn of release and something more profound—something growing.

The novelty of wanting him, of being wanted by him, hadn't worn off for six months.

It had only deepened. Seeped into the parts of me I thought would always stay locked.

This wasn't what I expected. Any of it.

With his quiet decency and devastating earnestness, Simon Radcliffe had slipped through my defenses like a tide, steady, patient, impossible to resist.

Not the kind that wrecks.

The kind that softens.

The kind that smooths out the rough places until you forget they were ever jagged.

His arms tightened around me, and his chest's steady rise and fall lulled me into a contented, dizzy haze.

We hadn't planned for the last six months. We hadn't planned any of this.

And maybe that was the best part of all.

***

Dear Reader,

Thank you so much for spending time with *Pleasure & Prose*. This story means the world to me—a quiet, burning love letter to unexpected vulnerability, slow-burning tension, and the kind of intimacy that sneaks up on you and refuses to let go.

Simon and Veronica couldn't be more different on the surface. But beneath the buttoned-up manners and carefully curated confidence are two people learning how to be seen—and loved—for exactly who they are. Writing their journey was messy, tender, a little steamy (okay, a lot steamy), and deeply satisfying. I hope it felt that way to you, too.

If you enjoyed your time in Briar Hill, I'd be so grateful if you left a review or told a fellow romance reader about the Thorne

Sisters series. Word of mouth is what helps small-town love stories like this find their way into new hearts. You can review the book here.

Thank you for reading. For feeling. For believing in cinnamon roll heroes and fiercely independent heroines. I can't wait to show you what's next.

With love and gratitude,

Hana York

***

Lessons & Leather

A steamy, small-town opposites-attract romance between a woman learning to want and a man learning he's wanted.

Hana York

Pink Pop Publishing

Lessons & Leather

(The Thorne Sisters Book 4)

Copyright © 2025 by Hana York

All rights reserved.

www.HanaYork.com

Contents

Prologue

ELIZA

The school parking lot was quiet when I pulled in—just a few scattered cars and the faint smell of mulch from the new flower beds.

I didn't turn off the engine right away.

Instead, I sat briefly, hands wrapped around my travel mug, steam curling against the windshield like a quiet reminder: you're okay. You're ready.

A tray of cupcakes wobbled in the passenger seat every time I breathed too hard. Twenty-four pink-frosted sugar bombs, each topped with a cherry gummy. A thank-you for the janitor. A pick-me-up for the front office. A treat for the kindergartners who spelled "hippopotamus" correctly yesterday, which was more than I could manage without spellcheck.

I nudged the tray toward the center of the seat, next to my tote bag bursting with construction paper and glitter glue. The bag slumped sideways, spilling a handful of googly eyes into the cup holder.

Of course it did.

I smiled. This was my version of chaos—glue sticks, snack schedules, and a running tally of which child had most recently eaten a crayon.

The smile faded.

Because underneath the glitter, cherry earrings, and extra napkins, there was this hum of something I couldn't name. A weight I'd carried so long it felt like mine.

I was good at being the reliable one. The cheerful one. The one who made everything easier.

But some mornings, I wondered what it would feel like to rely on someone else.

Not because I couldn't do it alone, but because I was tired of always having to.

And I hated that thought.

Because my sisters were my safety net, whether I admitted it or not.

Lola fought for me when I couldn't find the words.

Vivian dared me to live louder, even when I wanted to hide.

And Veronica always seemed to know what I needed. Gave me truth instead of comfort and reason to laugh when I wanted to cry.

They loved me. I knew that.

But sometimes... I still felt like the footnote in my own story.

I shook it off. Adjusted the radio. Slipped the car into drive.

And bumped straight into the back of the largest truck I'd ever seen.

My breath caught.

The tray of cupcakes lurched.

Pink frosting smudged.

No. No, no, no—

Where the heck did that thing come from?

I threw the car into park, grabbed napkins, and tried to clean it up, smearing frosting and nerves in equal measure.

The truck door opened, and a man stepped out.

Tall. Broad. Wearing a plain gray tee stretched over shoulders that should've come with a warning label.

He glanced at the back of his truck. Then at my car. Then at me.

And I knew—with total certainty—I was about to cry in front of someone who looked like he hadn't cried about anything in his entire life.

Wonderful.

Absolutely wonderful.

Chapter One

CLAY

The hit wasn't hard. Just enough to rock the truck and slosh half my coffee into the center console.

This was precisely why I avoided the school lot; there were too many minivans and distractions, and everyone was trying to do six things at once before eight a.m.

I exhaled through my nose. Counted to five.

Then I opened the door.

The car behind me was small. Pale blue. The front bumper barely nudged into mine like it regretted the decision halfway through.

Inside, the driver sat frozen.

Brown curls piled on top of her head in a loose bun. Big eyes, flushed cheeks, and a look of pure panic behind the windshield. I'd seen that face once or twice at pickup—Miss Thorne. Kindergarten teacher.

She looked horrified. Like she'd taken out my entire back end instead of tapping it at less than two miles an hour.

She stared at the steering wheel, as if hoping it might explain how this happened.

Then her gaze flicked to mine, and her whole face crumpled.

She climbed out slowly, eyes wide, hands fluttering like she wasn't sure what to do with them.

"I'm so sorry," she said, wringing her hands. "I looked down for one second to check on the cupcakes, and then there was a glitter spill. And now I'm here. In your truck."

She winced. "Not in your truck. Into. I bumped into your truck. Oh my god."

I said nothing.

Mostly because I didn't trust my mouth not to do something stupid.

Like smile.

She stepped closer, scanning the back of the truck like it might burst into flames at any second.

"Is it... bad? I don't see a dent. But that doesn't mean there isn't one. I mean, sometimes there's structural damage you can't see, right?"

She turned to me—earnest, hopeful, doomed.

I glanced at the bumper. Wiped my thumb along the edge where her license plate had tapped it.

"No damage."

"Oh. Thank god." She let out a breath, her hand pressing to her chest.

"I still feel awful." She glanced back at her car. "Can I offer you a cupcake? I brought extras."

Her voice wavered, like she wasn't sure if she was offering a treat or an apology.

"Vanilla with cherry buttercream. Some of them are a little—um, wonky. But they're still good."

There was glitter on her cheek. One lone sprinkle clinging to her blouse.

She winced. "Sorry. I ramble when I'm... well. This."

Her hand fluttered like she was trying to wave away the whole situation.

"I'm Eliza Thorne. I teach kindergarten here."

I nodded. "Clay Walker."

Her eyebrows lifted, waiting for more.

"Maggie's my niece. She's in your class."

Recognition bloomed fast. "Maggie! Of course. She's wonderful. So curious. She always asks the best questions."

"Yeah," I said. "That sounds like her."

Eliza smiled—soft and warm.

And something in my chest pulled tight.

I should've walked away.

Said "no damage." Got back in the truck.

But I didn't.

I just stood there like an idiot, watching her ramble about cupcakes with frosting on her fingers and glitter on her cheek.

I knew women like her. Sweet. Scattered. The kind who carried half the world on their shoulders and apologized when it got heavy.

Too bright. Too sweet. Too good for a man like me.

I knew what I looked like—big, broad, scruff on my jaw, grease under my nails. Ten years of mistakes and not a lot to show for them.

And around here, that's all people need. One glance and they think they've got me figured out.

Grumpy. Rough. Intimidating. Trouble if you're not careful.

They're not wrong.

And whatever this was—this pull?

It didn't matter.

Because women like her don't pick men like me.

And if they do, they don't stay.

She hesitated, then looked up at me with wide, hopeful eyes.

"I know there's no damage," she said, "but... can I still give you a cupcake?"

She tucked a curl behind her ear. "It would make me feel better."

And I should've said no.

I should've crossed my arms and done what people expected from someone like me.

But no one offered me cupcakes. Not without a smirk. Not without a joke about how I didn't look like the type who liked sweet things.

No one looked at me the way she did.

Like I wasn't a warning sign.

Like I was just... a man.

So I nodded. "Yeah. Sure."

Her whole face lit up—soft, like sunlight catching on glass.

She hurried back to the car, reached into the cupcake carrier, and carefully picked one. When she returned, she handed it to me like a peace offering. Or a promise.

"Still in one piece," she said. "Mostly."

I took it. Let my fingers brush hers, just for a second.

A spark. Small, stupid. Enough to short-circuit something in my chest.

"Thanks," I said gruffly. Like it was no big deal. Like it didn't matter.

But the way she looked at me? That was going to stay with me.

ELIZA

I tried to go about my day like I hadn't rear-ended the hottest man I'd ever seen.

Like he hadn't stepped out of that truck with broad shoulders, steady hands, and a voice that made *thanks* sound like a threat and a promise.

But I couldn't shake him.

Not through morning greetings, bulletin board prep, or even while answering an earnest question about whether dragons eat grilled cheese.

My thoughts kept circling back to him.

To the quiet way he watched me. The way his presence filled the space without taking it over.

To the impossible fact that a man like that—gruff, grounded, and built like a mountain—had looked at me like I wasn't just sweet. Like maybe I was something more.

And it was ridiculous.

I had twenty-four students, three parent emails to answer, and a glitter explosion still waiting in the supply closet. I did not have time for a crush.

The bell rang, and my classroom filled with tiny voices and oversized backpacks.

Greta was wearing her astronaut helmet again. Liam had already lost a shoe. Someone sneezed with the force of a cannon.

"Good morning, my brilliant beans," I said, clapping my hands. "Coats on hooks, bags in cubbies, then find your seat for morning meeting."

They shuffled into motion with the kind of semi-controlled chaos only kindergarten could produce.

I crouched to help Greta with her backpack zipper, and there it was again, that voice in my head.

Thanks.

Low. Rough. Just slightly surprised.

I stood too fast and bumped into the edge of my desk.

"Miss Thorne?"

Maggie Walker stood beside me, her backpack already hung, hands folded in front of her like the tiny old soul she was.

"Yes, Maggie?"

She tilted her head. "Are you okay? You look like you're thinking really hard."

I smiled. "Just a lot on my mind today."

She nodded. "Sometimes when I think too hard, I have to eat a snack."

Honestly? Not a bad plan.

"I'll keep that in mind. Thanks. Go find your spot on the rug."

She skipped away, and I took a deep breath, letting the hum of the classroom settle around me like armor.

***

By the time the last student had been picked up, the glitter spill contained, and my inbox mostly ignored, I was running on caffeine and cupcake fumes.

So, when Lola texted: *Thrift therapy? Meet us at The Lucky Rack?* I didn't hesitate.

Retail therapy with my sisters wasn't exactly relaxing, but it was comforting in its chaotic, opinion-heavy way.

And safer than going home and thinking about Clay Walker.

Lola was elbow-deep in a bin of vintage denim, muttering about someone ruining a perfectly good jacket with rhinestones. Vivian tried on oversized sunglasses in front of a cracked mirror, and Veronica was at the rack, fingers gliding over silk like she had all the time in the world.

I wandered toward the kitchenware section. There was something oddly comforting about mismatched mugs.

"You're quiet," Lola said without looking up. "That usually means you're overthinking something or planning to adopt a stray."

"Neither," I said. "Just... distracted."

Vivian raised an eyebrow. "By?"

I hesitated. "I may have... lightly rear-ended someone in the parking lot this morning."

All three of them looked up.

"Wait, what?" Veronica said. "Are you okay?"

"Fine. Barely a tap. No damage. He was very..." I searched for the right word: "understanding."

"Uh-huh," Vivian said slowly. "And?"

"And... hot."

That got their attention.

"Who was it?" Lola asked, instantly suspicious.

"Clay Walker," I said, trying to sound casual. Like it didn't matter. Like he hadn't been in my head all day.

Lola froze, her hand still tangled in denim. "Absolutely not."

I blinked. "What?"

She stood up, arms crossed. "He's too big. Too broody. Too rough. That man looks like he could break hearts just by breathing."

"That's dramatic," I said.

"It's accurate," she replied. "He doesn't do relationships—he does repairs, silence, and probably a lot of glaring."

Vivian adjusted her sunglasses. "He's... intense. Not uninteresting. But he might be too much for you."

I opened my mouth, but she held up a finger. "Not because you're fragile. But because you're kind. And men like him don't always know what to do with kindness."

Veronica leaned against a rack, one brow raised. "Or maybe kindness is exactly what he needs. And our sister's allowed to want a man who looks like he'd throw a wrench through a wall if someone hurt her."

Lola rolled her eyes. Vivian didn't argue.

Veronica looked at me. "You're allowed to want, Eliza. That's not a weakness."

I nodded. Quietly. Because I knew they meant well. I knew they loved me.

But how they said it—too rough, too intense, too much—felt familiar.

And for once, I didn't want to be the sweet one everyone worried would get hurt.

I wanted to be the kind of woman a man like Clay Walker couldn't look away from.

And for a moment this morning, I could almost believe I was.

Chapter Two

CLAY

Maple Hill Elementary smelled like sanitizer and fruit snacks.

Not exactly my comfort zone.

Too clean. Too bright. Too many memories of being told to sit still and quiet down.

But the school needed help. Budget cuts meant the janitor was covering too much, and someone had requested assistance with a broken swing and shelves in a kindergarten classroom.

I had time, I had tools, and I said yes a little too fast when they mentioned the room number.

12B.

Eliza's classroom.

I wasn't getting paid for this and didn't want to be.

Maggie was here. Eliza was here.

That was reason enough.

The secretary at the front handed me a note. "Everything you need should be in the supply closet."

I nodded and kept walking. Neat, rounded handwriting in purple ink.

Shelf in Room 12B. Swing on the east playground. Storage closet hinge. Thank you! – Eliza Thorne

I read it twice. Not because I didn't get it.

I shifted the weight of the toolbox and headed to her room.

Room 12B was supposed to be empty.

I'd timed it that way.

I figured the kids would be at lunch, and I could finish the shelves without getting in anyone's way.

But the second I stepped inside, I saw her.

Kneeling on the rug, hair slipping from her bun, fingers stained with green paint and glitter. Surrounded by paper scraps and kid-sized scissors.

And I felt that same low, steady pull I hadn't been able to shake since she rear-ended my truck and offered me a cupcake like it was a lifeline.

She looked up.

And I forgot why I was there.

"Mr. Walker?" she said, blinking like she wasn't sure I was real. Her eyes flicked to the toolbox, then back to my face. "Is everything okay?"

"Clay," I said. "Just Clay."

She straightened, smoothing her skirt with paint-streaked hands. "Okay... Clay."

"The office said the shelves in here needed fixing."

Her expression softened. "Oh—yes. That shelf's been threatening collapse for months. I wasn't expecting anyone today."

He shrugged. "There was a call for volunteers in the parent newsletter. My brother flagged it for me. Figured I had the tools. And the time."

Her brows lifted slightly. "You did?"

I nodded.

She smiled. And it did something dangerous to my resolve.

"Well... thank you. That's really kind of you."

I didn't know what to say, so I looked past her to a shelf leaning like it was too tired to stand straight.

"Shouldn't take long," I muttered.

"Want me to clear the area?" she asked, gathering glue sticks.

I shook my head. "You don't have to leave."

She paused. "Okay. I'll stay out of your way."

I didn't tell her I wouldn't mind the opposite.

I just knelt by the shelf and opened the toolbox, like I hadn't come here hoping to see her.

"I'm sorry the room's a mess," she said. "The kids are designing seed packets for the class garden. It's adorable in theory. In practice, it's chaotic."

I glanced at a piece of construction paper that said *SUN-FLOWER* in bubble letters, surrounded by glittery stickers and what looked like a vampire carrot.

"Looks like they're having fun."

"They are," she said, her whole face lighting up. "They love having something that's theirs, you know?"

I didn't, not really. But I nodded anyway.

"I knew you had the garage," she said. "But I didn't realize you fixed school shelves on your day off."

The fact that she knew anything about me settled deep in my chest, like a touch I didn't see coming.

I didn't let it show. Just shrugged. "They needed fixing."

Her smile tugged at the corner of her mouth. "You always this generous with your time?"

"No."

It came out flatter than I meant, but she didn't backpedal or get flustered.

"Need help holding anything? Not that I'm implying you can't do it alone," she added quickly. "You just look like you could use a second pair of hands."

I nodded, trying not to sound as affected as I felt. "All right. Hold the left side up for me."

She stepped in close enough that I caught the soft scent of vanilla and something floral.

When she lifted the shelf, our arms brushed, a subtle contact that sent a jolt straight through me.

She didn't flinch, but her breath hitched—just slightly.

Something shifted between us, in the air, in me.

She looked up, wide-eyed, lips parted like she might say something.

But she didn't.

And neither did I.

I just tightened my grip on the drill, anchored the bracket, and tried to focus on the work, not the way one brush of her skin had completely undone me.

ELIZA

He was close enough to rattle me completely.

His arm brushed mine as he anchored the shelf, and I could feel the heat rolling off him, steady and warm like sunlight after a storm.

I wanted to lean into it.

Curl into him like a cat and stay there.

Which was... alarming.

I tried to focus on the task, but all I could think about was how solid and warm he felt.

And then there was the smell of him.

Not cologne—nothing artificial. Just clean skin, warm cotton, the faint scent of cedar, heat, and something dangerous.

It did strange things to my body.

Unexpected things.

My heart beat faster. My breath hitched.

I swallowed hard and risked a glance at his face.

Focused. Calm. Like this was just another shelf on just another Tuesday.

I wasn't calm. Not even close.

And the worst part?

I didn't want to be.

He secured the last screw, gave the shelf a quick shake, then straightened.

"Should hold now," he said.

I nodded. "Looks great. Thank you."

He gave a slight shrug. "You're welcome." His eyes swept the room—the art projects, the glitter, the barely contained chaos. "Maggie says your classroom is crazy—but the good kind."

He paused, then added, "Feels like you've figured out how to make the chaos feel safe."

The words settled deep, unexpected, and steady.

People noticed the bright bulletin boards. The tidy cubbies. The songs, stickers, and smiles.

But not the effort beneath it. Not the way I worked to keep the chaos from swallowing the gentle parts.

And the way he looked at me—steady, warm, like he meant it—

It made my knees feel a little loose.

I smiled because it was the only thing I could think to do. "You're not so bad at steadying things yourself."

His mouth curved, just barely. "Different kind of mess."

I meant to say something back. Something light. Maybe even clever.

But the way he looked at me—steady, quiet, almost reverent—stopped the words in my throat.

The room felt suddenly still. Like the air between us had gone quiet.

He didn't look away.

And neither did I.

His gaze flicked down, just once, to my mouth.

And then he leaned in. Just a little.

I didn't move. Couldn't.

My heart thudded in my chest, loud enough to drown out thought.

And then—

Laughter echoed from the hallway.

We jumped apart like someone had flipped on a light.

Clay stepped back quickly, toolbox in hand.

The moment folded up between us like it hadn't happened at all.

He cleared his throat.

"I'm headed out to the playground," he said. "To look at that swing on your list."

I cleared my throat. "I can show you the way. It's tucked around the side, near the cafeteria."

He nodded. "Sounds good."

Clay walked beside me, steps steady, shoulders broad enough to block the sun if he tried.

We rounded the corner to the east playground, and he scanned the structure like he was already cataloging what needed attention.

"The swing's over there," I said, pointing. "One of the chains keeps catching."

He nodded and headed toward it.

I lingered nearby, watching him work without really meaning to.

And that's when I saw Max.

Perched at the top of the monkey bars, frozen halfway across.

He wasn't in my class, but I knew that look—panic creeping in, too proud to call for help.

Before I could take a step, Clay was already moving.

He didn't shout or panic.

Just walked over, calm and sure, and stopped at the base of the structure.

"You okay up there?" he asked, voice low and steady.

Max didn't answer. Just held on tighter.

Clay didn't push. Didn't crowd him.

He stood still, hands loose at his sides.

"You're doing great," he said. "Take your time."

His voice dropped a little, softer now. "I've gotten stuck before, too."

That was all it took.

Max exhaled, scooted forward one bar at a time, and reached the platform.

Clay held out a hand. No pressure. No urgency.

Just there. Just steady.

And when Max took it, something in my chest squeezed tight.

Because yes, Clay Walker was big. Brooding. Looked like he could crush a wrench with one hand.

But I'd just watched him coax a scared kid down from the monkey bars without raising his voice or breaking a sweat.

And no matter what people in town said about him...

I knew better now.

Chapter Three

CLAY

The kid's hand was small in mine.

Sweaty. Shaky.

But he held on.

Didn't cry. Didn't panic. Just breathed through it—step by step—until he was back on solid ground.

"Nice work," I said quietly.

He nodded and took off toward the picnic tables as if nothing had happened.

I watched him go. Made sure his shoulders uncurled. His pace evened out.

When I turned, Eliza watched me with an admiration I wasn't sure I'd earned.

Like what I'd just done hadn't surprised her.

Like it had confirmed something she already believed.

That I was good.

And I couldn't remember the last time anyone had looked at me like that.

It hit harder than that almost-kiss in her classroom.

***

The swing wasn't complicated—just a kinked chain and a loose bolt. Fifteen minutes of easy work.

But I couldn't stop thinking about her. The way she hadn't flinched when I leaned in. The way she'd looked at me, like I was something steady. Something worth admiring.

I should've felt steady, too.

Instead, I drove back to the shop, my grip too tight on the wheel, and my thoughts too loud to ignore.

The garage was quiet when I got there.

Concrete floors. Humming lights. Tools right where I left them.

I used to like the stillness.

Today, it felt too empty.

I wiped down the bench. Checked the inventory clipboard.

Tried to shake her voice from the back of my mind.

Then came the telltale thud of boots against concrete.

Tanner.

He didn't knock. Just walked in, grabbed a root beer from the fridge, and leaned against the counter like this was a social call.

"Lola mentioned the fender bender," he said casually.

I wiped my hands on a rag. "She barely tapped my bumper."

"Right," he smirked. "And then gave you a cupcake."

I didn't answer.

He took a sip, watching me. "Just so we're clear—Lola's already sharpening knives. So if you're gonna mess around with Eliza..."

"I'm not."

He raised an eyebrow.

I didn't flinch. "I'm not."

Tanner leaned back, slow and easy. "Okay. Then what are you doing?"

I returned to wiping down the same wrench I'd already cleaned twice.

"She's... nice," I said finally. "Kind."

He laughed under his breath. "Yeah, Clay. She's also a grown woman. Not a rescue dog."

"She looked at me like I was... good," I muttered. "Like I wasn't someone to be avoided."

There was a pause before Tanner said, "Maybe that's because you are good."

I shook my head. "Not the kind of good she deserves."

"You let her decide that."

He finished the root beer and set the bottle down with a soft clink.

He turned to me with a look that was steady, serious. No trace of his usual grin.

"Look. I know what people in this town say about you. And I know that's all bullshit."

I didn't move.

"But Eliza?" His voice dropped. "She's not just Lola's sister. She's *Eliza*. You hurt her, even by accident, you're not just answering to me. You're answering to three very protective sisters. And trust me, they're a hell of a lot scarier than me, man."

He paused and then added, "So if you're in, be in. And if you're not... walk away now."

He didn't wait for an answer.

Just gave me one last look and walked out.

The garage door creaked shut behind him.

And the silence settled back in.

But for once, I didn't know what the hell to do with it.

ELIZA

I didn't mean to cry.

I told myself I just needed to grab more glue sticks.

But really, I needed a minute.

Just one quiet minute.

The supply closet was cool, cramped, and smelled like old paper and lemon cleaner. I sat on the floor beside a box of construction paper, blinking hard at the shelves, trying not to cry.

A parent had stopped me in the hall this afternoon.

"You're adorable," she'd said, with a smile that didn't quite reach her eyes. "The kids must think of you like a big sister. Hopefully, they'll have a *real* teacher next year to keep them on track."

The words clung to me like glitter. Light on the surface. Impossible to shake.

I'd smiled, like I always do. Nodded. Said thank you.

And then I hid in the supply closet.

I *was* young, sweet, smiley, and glittery.

But I was more than that.

I was also the kind of teacher who made up songs about handwashing and stayed up late cutting bulletin board flowers.

The kind who built lesson plans from scratch, met with parents after hours, read education journals, and worried about my students as if it were a second job.

And I was tired—bone-deep tired-of being treated like a Pinterest board in a cardigan.

The tears came faster now, no matter how hard I blinked.

So I curled in on myself, arms around my knees, and tried to ride it out.

Which, of course, was when the door opened.

I stiffened. Swiped at my cheeks.

"Sorry—just grabbing—" The voice stopped me cold.

"Miss Thorne?"

Clay.

Of course.

I scrambled to my feet too fast, knocking into a crate of dry erase markers. "Hi! Sorry—I was just..."

He stepped in, frowning gently. "They told me the hinge in here needed fixing. Didn't think anyone would be inside."

I stood quickly, brushing my skirt. "Sorry. I didn't mean to be in the way."

He glanced at the crate. The tissues in my hand. My blotchy face.

"You okay?"

I nodded. Then, I shook my head.

And the tears came all over again.

Clay didn't say anything.

He just stepped forward, calm and confident, and closed the door behind him.

Then, without asking, without hesitating, he wrapped his arms around me.

No questions. Just warm, solid comfort.

I froze for a beat. Then melted into him like I belonged there.

He held me like it was the easiest thing in the world.

And for the first time all day, I could breathe.

His chest was warm beneath my cheek, rising and falling in a rhythm that calmed me.

No one had ever held me like this before.

Like I wasn't a burden. Like I didn't have to apologize for needing this.

And somewhere between the weight of his arms and the quiet strength of his presence, the tears began to slow.

I breathed in slowly and deeply, and didn't pull away.

Instead, I whispered the only thing I could manage. "Thank you."

He didn't answer.

I leaned back to look at him, and that's when I saw it.

It wasn't just concern. Or kindness. There was something deeper in his eyes—something that looked a lot like want.

He didn't speak or move.

But the air between us shifted, electric and still.

I slid my hand to his chest, right over his heart. It was racing. So was mine.

And then he kissed me.

Not cautiously. Not like he was testing the moment.

Like he'd been carrying the want of it for miles and finally let it break free.

His mouth met mine with a heat that stole my breath, with a tenderness that made me ache.

His hand slid to the back of my neck, fingers threading into my hair, steady, sure, and a little bit reverent.

I curled into him, fists clutching the worn fabric of his shirt, like maybe if I held tight enough, I could keep this moment from slipping away.

The kiss was deep. Consuming. The kind you only get once—the kind that says, *You matter. You're wanted. You're real.*

And when he sighed into my mouth—low and rough, all unraveling control—I felt something inside me break open.

Not painfully.

But with relief.

Like this wasn't just a kiss.

It was a beginning.

And I would never forget it.

Chapter Four

CLAY

I'd kissed women before. Plenty.

But nothing like this.

This wasn't just heat or sweetness—it was trust.

The way she leaned into me, like I was something steady, something safe. Like she believed I could handle her trust, and wanted me to have it.

That's what undid me.

Not the softness of her lips or how her fingers curled into my shirt.

It was the way she gave me this moment, unguarded.

Like she didn't doubt for a second that I'd take care of it.

She sighed into my mouth, low and quiet, and I felt it everywhere. In my chest. My gut. My hands twitched at my sides, itching to pull her closer.

I wanted more.

More of that sound. More of her, wrapped around me like a secret I hadn't earned but couldn't let go of. More of the way she tilted her face like she already knew how I kissed and wanted every inch of it.

I could've lost myself right there—

Would've, if she'd made one more sound like that.

If she'd pulled me even a breath closer, I wouldn't have stopped.

But Eliza Thorne didn't deserve a rushed moment in a supply closet.

She wasn't a fleeting thing.

And I didn't want to be the kind of man who treated her like one.

So I pulled back, just enough to breathe.

She blinked up at me, kiss-drunk and flushed, and it nearly broke my resolve.

"I should go," I said, my voice rough around the edges.

Her hand was still on my chest.

Stepping back felt like tearing something essential from my skin.

"I'll fix the hinge next time." Then I turned and walked out.

Because if I stayed, I was going to forget where we were. Forget everything but her body against mine, and the way she came undone in my arms.

***

The beer sat on the counter, half-warm and untouched. I'd pulled it from the fridge over an hour ago, cracked it open, taken a sip, and never gone back. Now it just sat there, sweating.

The house was quiet. Too quiet.

No music. No engine hum. No Maggie asking if I could fix her scooter again. Just me, and the kiss I couldn't stop replaying.

Her lips. Her fingers curled in my shirt. That soft, impossible sigh.

I'd felt it everywhere. And now I couldn't get it out of my head.

I closed my eyes and tried to shake it, but it didn't work. I could still feel the weight of her pressed into me, the heat, the way she didn't pull away. The way she looked at me when I did.

Not angry. Not confused. Just... open. Like she trusted me to do the right thing.

And I had, maybe.

Because the truth was, I didn't know how to be what she needed. Not really.

She deserved someone steady. Someone who didn't stumble over his own silences or second-guess every word.

Someone who didn't carry ten years of silence in his bones.

I looked down at my hands—rough, calloused, scarred from a dozen engines and a thousand hours of work.

Hands that were good at fixing things.

But I didn't know if they were good at holding on.

Especially to someone like Eliza Thorne.

Someone who made the world softer.

Who made me want things I hadn't let myself want in a long time.

Didn't matter.

Because I already knew the truth.

I was falling.

And the only question now was whether I was brave enough to land.

I didn't know how to sit with this kind of wanting.

Didn't know what to do with the way my body felt coiled and hot.

I'd pulled back from her. Walked out. Done what I thought was right.

And now I was alone, with nothing but my own indecision.

I sighed. Turned off the kitchen light.

The bedroom wasn't much better—just a bed, a dresser, and a few shirts draped over the chair.

But it was dark. Quiet.

A little less like standing in the middle of a decision I didn't know how to make.

I sat on the edge of the bed. Rubbed a hand over the scruff on my jaw.

Then I lay back. Closed my eyes.

It was a losing battle.

Trying not to think about her.

That kiss.

She'd leaned in, soft and certain, like I was something good.

My breath hitched. My body tightened.

I thought about her mouth. Her small fingers tugging at my shirt. That sound she made—the low, sweet sigh that went straight to my gut.

I groaned out loud.

How the hell was I this desperate when I'd barely even touched her?

My hands trembled as I unfastened the button on my jeans. The zipper followed—loud in the quiet room.

I freed my cock, the cool air a jolt across flushed skin.

I was hard. So fucking hard.

I bit back a groan and wrapped my hand around the ache.

I stroked slowly at first, grip firm, the rhythm steady.

A bead of pre-cum slid from the tip. I used it, dragging my palm over the head.

My hips rocked, instinct driving the pace.

I thought about Eliza.

The curve of her neck.

The softness under my hands.

The way she'd look if I were inside her—wide-eyed and flushed, holding on tight.

My hand moved faster, grip tightening as I chased the high I could already feel building.

A strangled moan tore from my throat. I didn't try to stop it, my hips jerking as the tension coiled tight.

One more stroke. One more second and I came hard.

The release hit like a punch rolling through me in crashing waves.

I gasped, sweat beading along my spine.

And when it passed, when the last tremor faded, I knew one thing for sure.

This wasn't even close to what it would feel like with her.

But damn if I didn't want to find out.

ELIZA

After school, I headed straight to Pleasure & Co.

I needed to talk to Veronica.

And it needed to be in person.

She looked up as soon as I walked in, sharp eyes catching mine over the rim of a clipboard.

"That's a face," she said. "What happened?"

I hesitated near the counter, fingers curling in the hem of my cardigan.

"I kissed him," I said.

Veronica blinked. "Well. Okay then. Come on."

She guided me to the back room and poured two glasses of wine.

And just like that, I started talking.

"Clay's been helping out at the school," I said. "Fixing stuff. Shelves, playground equipment. I guess the office called in a favor, and he showed up."

Veronica gave me a knowing look. "Uh-huh."

I tucked a knee up on the velvet loveseat and stared at my wine glass.

"I was in the supply closet. A parent said something that really got to me—told me I was adorable. Said the kids probably think of me as a big sister. That maybe next year they'd get a *real* teacher to keep them on track."

Veronica's mouth tightened, but she didn't interrupt.

"I didn't cry in front of her. I smiled. Nodded. Said thanks." I let out a breath. "But the second I was alone, I broke."

Veronica leaned back, her expression softening.

"I thought I was alone," I said. "Then Clay came in—he was supposed to fix the door hinge, and he found me on the floor, trying to get it together."

I could still feel the weight of his arms.

"He didn't say anything. Just closed the door and held me."

Veronica's brows lifted slightly.

"I've never been held like that before. Like I was allowed to fall apart."

The tears that pricked now weren't from pain. They were from the memory of safety.

"And then I looked up at him... and he kissed me."

Veronica didn't say a word.

"It wasn't rushed. It wasn't soft, either. It was—God. It was everything. I felt it everywhere. But the second I leaned into it, he pulled back. Said he had to go."

I shook my head. "And I just... I don't know how to be what he wants. I want him to want me. I want him to look at me like he can't help it. But I don't know how to get there."

Veronica didn't rush to answer. She set her glass down and waited for my eyes to meet hers.

"Sweetheart," she said, "you don't need to figure out how to be wanted. You already are."

"I want to be myself," I said. "I just... I've never done this before. Not any of it. I'm a virgin."

Veronica didn't rush to speak. She set her glass down and met my gaze, steady as ever.

"You're the only one I've ever told," I added. "Not even the others know. I didn't want them to think I was some delicate little girl who needed to be protected. You've all lived and loved and made bold choices. And I've just... been safe."

She reached for my hand and held it.

"You don't need experience to be desirable," she said. "You need honesty. Presence. Trust. You already have those in spades. And if Clay Walker has half a brain in that broody, brawny head of his—he's already half in love with you and doesn't know what to do about it."

I let out a shaky laugh.

Veronica smiled and leaned back. "Let yourself want this. That's the boldest thing you can do."

I glanced over at her. "Can I ask you something?"

Veronica raised a brow. "Eliza, you can ask me anything."

"I know I want to be with him. Intimately. On some deep level, I know that." I hesitated. "But the truth is... I don't really know what that means. Not fully."

Veronica's expression softened. 'You don't have to know everything to know what you want.'

I nodded slowly, the words catching in my throat.

"I've never been with anyone. Not even close. I've never made out with someone. Never... taken care of things on my own." My face warmed, but I kept going. "I've never explored that side of myself at all."

I shook my head. "And it feels like there's this whole world I'm supposed to just know how to navigate. But I don't. I don't even know what I like. So how can I even think about being with someone else if I haven't figured out any of that?"

Veronica's expression softened—not with pity, but with something close to admiration.

"Eliza," she said gently, "you don't have to know everything. You just have to be willing to learn yourself. That's where it starts—not with anyone else. With you. What feels good. What feels right. What feels like you."

I let out a shaky breath.

She leaned forward, voice low and sure. "You don't need permission to explore that side of yourself—and you sure as hell don't need to be experienced to deserve intimacy."

Veronica stood, crossed the room, and opened a small cabinet near the back wall.

She didn't say anything at first. Just sifted through the shelves like she was choosing a bottle of wine or the right shade of lipstick.

She turned back with a small satin bag in her hand.

"This isn't about the toy," she said, placing it gently in my lap. "It's about the choice. About giving yourself permission to figure out what you like—what feels good, what feels true. This is just one way in."

My fingers curled around the bag.

It was soft. Light. A little intimidating.

But mostly it felt like possibility.

I looked up. "What if I mess it up?"

Veronica smiled. "Eliza. You can't mess up pleasure. You can only ignore it. And you've done that long enough."

Something loosened in my chest.

Maybe it was the weight of all the years I'd spent waiting.

Maybe it was the quiet realization that I no longer had to wait.

Chapter Five

ELIZA

When I got to my apartment, I locked the door and set the bag on the bed.

Then I changed out of my school clothes and pulled on something soft and loose.

No music. No distractions. Just the quiet. And me.

For the first time, I didn't feel like I was waiting. I was present—in my body, in my choice, in the quiet pull of something I was finally ready to want.

I was nervous, but I lay back on my bed and let my fingers trail over my skin.

Tentative at first, I touched myself in a way I never had. My hands skimmed upward, teasing the curve of my breasts through the fabric, and I gasped when I brushed a nipple. The sensation lit me up, a delicious shiver running through me. I did it again—circling, pressing—feeling my nipples harden under my touch. I pinched one lightly and moaned, the sound foreign and wholly mine.

My body responded instantly. A rush of wet heat pooled low between my legs, making me ache in a way that felt both raw and thrilling. I'd never known this kind of pleasure. This kind of wonder.

I thought of Clay. His hands. His mouth. The way he kissed me like I was something sacred. Everything inside me tightened.

My breath quickened, and my fingers moved with more urgency. I squeezed and pinched, chasing the sweet, pulsing heat that had bloomed in my belly.

The ache between my legs was intense now, my panties damp, the fabric clinging to my swollen flesh. I arched off the bed, thighs pressing together.

My hand trembled as I reached for the toy, the satin bag sending a thrill up my spine. I opened it, breathless.

A clit simulator.

I slipped off my panties and settled back against the pillows. The cool air kissed my bare skin, making me shiver.

I held the toy in my hand. Read the instructions twice. Then pressed it to my clit and turned it on.

The first hum made me gasp, low and desperate.

The vibration was intense. I dialed it back, easing in. My hips lifted instinctively as I adjusted the setting, finding a rhythm that matched my racing heart.

I moaned, wet and throbbing, my body moving with the toy's pulse.

I pictured Clay. His hands on my hips. His mouth at my throat. His eyes dark with want.

A fresh wave of heat tore through me.

My thighs trembled. I tilted my hips with each thrust, the friction exact and perfect. The pleasure burned low and deep, coiling tighter.

I came with a cry, loud and breathless.

The orgasm ripped through me—hot, consuming, endless. Wave after wave crashed over me, each pulse stronger than the last.

I gasped, body trembling, the aftershocks leaving me raw and aching in the best way.

I hadn't known I could feel like this. So free. So full.

I lay there, breathless. Limbs heavy. Skin flushed.

I didn't feel new. Or changed. Just... more.

More present. More in tune with myself.

I'd touched something quiet and private—and now I wanted more.

More curiosity. More pleasure.

More of the spark Clay had stirred awake in me.

And I didn't want to wait.

CLAY

It was just past six when I locked up the front bay.

The air was cooling, but the place smelled like heat and engine grease.

I'd wiped down the tools, swept the floor, and told myself to head home.

But I didn't move.

I was still at the counter when the bell over the door chimed.

Probably forgot to lock up. Probably someone needing a jump.

But when I turned—it was Eliza.

She stood just inside the door, one hand hooked around the strap of her bag. Her hair was pinned up, wisps catching the light, and she wore a sweater the color of sun-warmed honey. Her expression was soft, steady, like she'd made up her mind and wasn't backing down.

My pulse hit like a misfired spark.

"I hope I'm not interrupting," she said.

"You're not." My voice came out rougher than I meant.

She stepped forward. Not shy. Not rushed. Just sure.

"I thought about waiting," she said. "But then I realized I didn't want to."

I stared.

"I've been doing that most of my life—waiting. To be ready. To be wanted. To feel like enough." Her eyes locked on mine. "But I'm not waiting anymore."

I swallowed hard.

"Eliza..."

She smiled—half bold, half uncertain. "You keep looking at me like I'm made of glass. I'm not."

I didn't move.

She came closer. Close enough that I felt that pull again.

"I'm not asking for perfect," she whispered. "I'm asking for real. For you."

I'd spent years keeping people at arm's length, thinking I was doing them a favor. But she didn't want space. She wanted me. And just like that, every excuse I'd clung to fell apart.

She stepped in further, looking at me like she already knew.

So I reached for her.

My hands settled at her waist, hesitant for half a second—until she leaned in, soft and certain—and then I was done.

I kissed her.

Not carefully or with caution, but with want.

With everything I hadn't let myself say.

Her hands slid under my shirt, fingers brushing skin, and she sighed against my mouth—soft, low, a sound that lit every nerve I had.

I backed her toward the counter, one slow step at a time, until her lower back met the edge of the wood.

She didn't pull away. Didn't hesitate or second-guess. She was here, choosing me, and I had never wanted anything more.

I kissed down her neck, lingering at the soft spot below her ear. She shivered under my touch, her hands fisting in my shirt, pulling me closer.

"Come here," I muttered against her skin, pulling back just enough to look into her eyes.

She nodded. Breathless. Ready.

I took her hand, led her through the side door, and into the office.

I pushed aside a stack of invoices, lifted her onto the desk, and slipped my hands beneath her sweater.

Her skin was soft and warm.

When I brushed my thumb over her nipple, she arched into me, a soft moan spilling from her lips.

I kissed her hard.

"Eliza." My voice was rough. "I want to taste you. Is that alright?"

Her breath hitched. "Yes. God, yes."

I kissed my way down her body—slow and sure—savoring the heat of her skin. Her ribs. Her stomach. The delicate curve of her hip.

Her head tipped back, lips parted, another needy sound escaping her that went straight to my cock.

I hooked my fingers under her panties and slid them down. Her breath shuddered out, quick, eager.

She was bare before me.

The most beautiful thing I'd ever seen.

I knelt, lifted one of her legs over my shoulder, and took in the sight before me.

Chapter Six

CLAY

Her scent hit me first—musky and sweet. I groaned, the sound vibrating against her skin. She was slick with want, and the first taste of her sent a jolt through my whole body.

Fuck. She was perfect.

Better than anything I'd ever imagined. I licked and sucked, slow at first, then faster as her hips bucked and her fingers tangled in my hair.

Her breath came fast, her thighs trembling against my shoulders.

My cock throbbed, painfully hard, but I didn't stop.

Wouldn't.

I wanted her to fall apart. Wanted to be the one who made it happen.

Her grip on my hair tightened. "Clay," she gasped—half plea, half demand. "More. I need more."

I slid a finger inside her, slow and careful.

Christ. She was tight.

She clenched around me, and I bit back a groan. Her body yielded, opening, until I felt it—her barrier.

Shock punched through me.

She was a virgin.

I almost stopped, but then she whimpered, her legs tightening, and I couldn't leave her hanging—not when she was so close.

I eased my finger back in, and she arched, moaning her pleasure.

I added another finger, stretching her gently, working her open and continued to lick her clit. It was swollen and throbbing, and I knew she was close, so close.

Her hips bucked against my mouth, the desk creaking beneath her. I fucked her with my fingers, careful not to breach that which I didn't have permission to take.

I could feel her climbing as her pussy tightened even more around my fingers.

And all I could think about was what it would feel like to sink into her. To be her first.

My hips rocked, instinctive, driven by the thought.

But I held myself back.

Because I wanted her to come. To feel the pleasure I could bring her.

"Clay," she cried. "I—" Her words broke.

I sucked her clit harder, fingers driving steady and sure and she shattered.

Her body arched off the desk, her cry sharp, sweet, and endless. I didn't stop. Stayed with her, fingers deep, mouth still moving, catching every aftershock, every pulse.

She slumped, breathless and glowing.

The most beautiful thing I'd ever seen.

I rose, gathered her into my arms. Her skin burned against mine, her chest rising and falling in a shaky rhythm.

I kissed her. She melted into it, soft and sweet.

Her arms wrapped around my neck. Fingers in my hair.

And I knew there was no coming back from this.

ELIZA

I couldn't breathe. Couldn't think. Couldn't believe how hard I'd just come.

The toy had been amazing—a revelation—but this?

This was ten thousand times better.

Clay's mouth, his hands, his everything had undone me, and I wasn't sure I'd ever be put back together.

I thought I knew what it meant to want, to feel, to be alive in my body.

Now, I realized I knew nothing.

Nothing but how impossibly good this was.

A stunned laugh bubbled out of me. I reached for him, needing to know he was real.

I kissed him and tasted myself on his tongue. Clay groaned low in his throat, cupped my face with both hands, and deepened the kiss. He kissed like he couldn't get enough, and my whole body responded—hungry for more.

"Clay," I whispered, breathless. "I can't believe how..." I flushed, heat blooming at the memory. "I didn't know it could feel like that."

His mouth curved into a wicked grin. "And that was just my mouth."

Heat pooled low in my belly again, want coiling tight.

"I want more," I said, meaning every word. "I want you."

I pulled him closer, fingers curled in his shirt.

Clay's hands stilled, eyes searching mine. Hesitant. Uncertain.

"You're a virgin," he said—not a question, not an accusation.

"Does that disappoint you?" My voice came out small, unsure.

He blinked. "What? No. Fuck, no." His hands rose to cradle my face, gentle and reverent. "Christ, Eliza. That just makes me want to earn every part of this. Every part of you."

My heart swelled—relief, desire, maybe even hope.

He didn't pull away. Didn't stop looking at me like I was the best thing that had ever happened to him.

"More than anything," he said, voice low and steady, "I want to be the one you trust with that. I want to be with you. More than I've ever wanted anything."

His breath was warm against my skin. "But not here. Not in the office. Not when I'm this close to losing my head."

I blinked, trying to follow.

He leaned in and kissed me again; this time, it felt like a promise.

"I want your first time to be somewhere special," he murmured, voice rough. "Not on my desk."

The warmth in my chest flickered and cooled. "So... you don't want to?"

He pulled back, the loss of contact like a slap of cold air.

"No," he said. "I mean—yes. I mean—"

My heart dropped.

He let out a ragged breath. "Eliza, I want you so fucking bad. That's why I'm trying to—"

But the doubt was already there. Burrowed deep.

I didn't hear the rest—not really. Because by then, I already knew where this was going.

He was pulling back again. Hesitating.

And I couldn't stand still and wait for it this time.

I slid off the desk, gathering the scattered pieces of myself—my shirt, my composure, the sting of wanting something I wasn't sure I was allowed to have.

"Thanks for... this," I said, my voice quiet as I crossed to the door. "I should go."

I didn't look at him. I didn't trust myself to.

Because the truth was already sinking in—too heavy, too familiar.

I was too much and not enough, all at once.

And he couldn't even say it.

Not clearly. Not without flinching.

My hand found the doorknob. I took a breath, steadying myself.

"See you around, Clay."

"Fuck," he said. "Eliza, wait—"

But I didn't.

I turned the knob, kept my head down, and walked out before he could see me cry.

I cursed my own stupidity as I drove home.

What had I expected?

That he'd be so overwhelmed with desire he'd take me right there, on his desk?

That he'd lose all control? That he'd want me so much he couldn't stop?

Maybe. Maybe that's precisely what I'd expected.

And maybe... I was more naive than I thought.

Chapter Seven

CLAY

I had to go after her before I lost my mind. Before she lost faith in me completely.

Because Eliza had it all wrong, and I needed to prove it.

The desk was still a mess. Her cardigan was on the floor. My hands were shaking.

I could still taste her on my tongue.

"Fuck," I muttered, staring at the empty doorway like it might spit her back out if I stood there long enough.

She thought I didn't want her.

Thought I was hesitating because of her.

Not because I wanted her so much, I could barely think.

I hadn't meant to hurt her. Jesus, I'd been trying to protect her. To make it right.

And I still managed to fuck it up.

I didn't even realize I'd pulled out my phone until it was already ringing.

Tanner picked up on the second ring. "Hey, man—"

"I need your help."

"What's going on? You okay?"

"No." I let out a breath. "I screwed up."

"What happened?"

"I said the wrong thing. Or maybe the right thing, but in the wrong way. She left. And I need to find her. But I don't know where she lives."

Another pause. Longer.

"You're talking about Eliza."

"Yeah."

He hesitated. "You hurt her?"

I gritted my teeth. "Not on purpose. But yeah. I think I did."

A sigh. "Clay—Lola's gonna skin you."

"I know. I don't care. Just tell me where she is so I can fix it."

Tanner was quiet for another moment.

"You better mean that."

"I do." My voice came out low. Honest. "She's the best thing that's ever happened to me. I'm not letting her walk away thinking I didn't want her."

Another beat.

Then Tanner gave me the address.

"Good luck," he said.

I was gonna need it.

I didn't wait to change. Just grabbed my keys, locked up, and got on my motorcycle.

The whole drive there, my mind spun.

What if she didn't open the door?

What if she didn't believe me?

I'd never chased anyone before.

Didn't know how to say the right thing, or how to fix something I broke with words instead of tools.

But I knew this, I wasn't letting her go without a fight.

When I pulled up to the address, the lights were on in the upstairs apartment.

I took the steps two at a time and knocked.

Nothing.

Knocked again. Firmer this time. "Eliza?"

Still nothing.

My chest tightened. I rubbed a hand down the back of my neck, about to knock again, when the door finally opened.

She stood barefoot, a soft cardigan over a tank top, her hair down, like she'd pulled it loose in frustration. Or exhaustion.

Her eyes were red like she'd been crying.

"Eliza," I breathed. "I'm sorry."

She didn't move at first.

"I need to explain," I said, my voice rough. "Just give me a minute. That's all I'm asking."

Still silent, she didn't slam the door—or speak. Instead, she opened it wider and stepped back.

I followed her inside, the air thick between us.

And right then, I made myself a promise: I was going to say every goddamn thing I should've said before she walked away.

I could've started with *I didn't mean it like that* or *You've got it all wrong.*

But that would've just been armor.

And I didn't want armor anymore.

Not with her.

So I said the only thing that mattered.

"I want you."

That got her eyes on mine.

"I want you so much it scares the hell out of me." I stepped closer. "And not because you're fragile. It's because you're real, and kind, and generous, and sexy as hell. And because you look at me like I'm more than the worst things people think about me."

Her mouth parted slightly, but she didn't interrupt.

"I'm not good at this," I said. "Saying the right thing. Doing the right thing. Growing up, there wasn't a lot of talking. No softness. No trust. You kept your head down and tried not to get in the way."

I scrubbed a hand through my hair.

"And I started believing I was the kind of man people tolerate. Not the kind they choose. But you make me feel like the man I've been trying to be was in there all along. Like maybe I just needed someone to see him."

I swallowed hard.

"I pulled back because I didn't want to mess it up. Because it meant something. *You* mean something. And I didn't want your first time to be a regret you carry."

Her expression shifted—something between hope and hesitation.

"I didn't pull back because I didn't want you." My voice dropped. "I pulled back because I want you too much."

I stepped closer, slow and steady.

"And if you still want me after this... I swear, I'm not going anywhere."

ELIZA

I uncrossed my arms. Stepped forward. Slowly.

I thought you were pulling away because you didn't want me." I said quietly.

His brow furrowed. "Eliza—"

"I know. That's not what you said." I looked up at him. "It's just... I've spent a long time feeling like I'm too much in all the wrong ways. Or not enough in the ways that count. And when you hesitated, even for a second... I heard every fear I've ever had."

His jaw tightened—not in anger, but in understanding.

"I thought you were rejecting me," I said, softer now. "And I ran before you could."

His chest rose, like he was holding something in. Maybe guilt. Maybe relief. Maybe both.

"I get why you wanted to slow things down," I said. "I just... needed to know you still wanted me."

"I do," he said, without hesitation. "I never stopped."

I reached out, brushing my fingers over the front of his shirt, slow and sure.

"Then stay."

My voice was so quiet I almost couldn't hear it over my heartbeat. "Please, Clay. Stay with me tonight."

I kissed him, soft at first, then full of all the longing I'd held back. He groaned into my mouth, a raw, rough sound that sent a thrill through me. His hands found my waist, pulling me close, grounding me, showing me this was real.

He backed me toward the bedroom, our bodies moving in a clumsy, hungry dance, neither of us willing to break the kiss until the backs of my knees hit the bed.

We went down together, his weight and warmth pressing into me. A soft moan escaped when I felt the full length of his cock hard against my thigh.

He caught himself on his elbows, his breath hot against my cheek. "Are you sure?" he asked, voice low, eyes locked on mine.

A wild, reckless joy bloomed in my chest.

"Oh my god, yes," I breathed. "I've never been more sure of anything."

Clay let out a shaky exhale. Then he kissed me again—deep and desperate—as his hands slid beneath my cardigan, pushing it off my shoulders before tugging my tank top up and over my head.

The cool air hit my skin, and I shivered, arching into him as he cupped my breasts, kneading them through the thin lace of my bra. My nipples tightened under his thumbs, and he groaned, his mouth finding mine again as I gasped.

Then he moved lower, his mouth replacing his hands. He sucked gently through the lace, his teeth grazing the peaks, and I moaned—a high, breathless sound.

"Please," I whispered, pulling him up to meet my eyes. "I want to feel you. All of you."

He reached behind me, unhooked my bra, and tossed it aside.

My body arched toward him, desperate and aching.

He growled low, the sound raw and full of promise, then lowered his mouth to my breast, sucking me into a wet, hot heat that shattered my breath.

My fingers threaded through his hair.

"Yes," I gasped as he moved to the other side, teasing the hardened peak with his tongue and teeth.

"Clay—yes."

The sensation was exquisite. Almost too much. A rush of need pooled between my legs, urgent and hot.

I tugged at his shirt, desperate to feel his skin against mine. He sat back, pulling it off in one smooth motion, and my hands flew to him, over the broad expanse of chest and muscle, memorizing him.

He was beautiful. Mine.

His eyes met mine, dark and molten. Then he lowered himself back over me, the thick length of him pressing hot and hard against my core, making my whole body come alive.

I wound my arms around his neck, hips rocking up against him, legs wrapping around his waist.

I could feel him—hard and insistent—and I wanted him inside me. Stretching. Filling. Claiming.

My fingers fumbled at the button of his jeans, trembling with need. With hunger. With the wild certainty that this was it. That *he* was it.

Clay's breath caught. He drew back slightly, his voice rough with restraint.

"Eliza, I'm big. And you're a virgin. I don't want to hurt you."

I blinked, heart skipping. "What?"

His face was tight, careful. "You're so small. And I'm... not. I need to get you ready first."

Relief and desire slammed through me, flooding every part of me.

He wasn't pulling away. He was protecting me.

"Clay, what if you don't..." My voice dropped. "What if you don't fit?"

The words barely made it out. I felt ridiculous saying them, but the fear was real. I'd never done this before.

His eyes darkened, and he made a low, guttural sound that sent heat spiraling through me.

He cupped my cheek, his voice low and steady.

"We'll make it work," he said. "I want this to be good for you, Eliza. I want it to be perfect."

Chapter Eight

CLAY

I kissed her again, slow and deep, letting her feel everything—my want, my certainty, my promise to take my time. I wasn't going to rush. I wasn't going to hurt her. I was going to make sure she was ready for me. Every inch of her.

I wanted her wet and wanting. I wanted to push her to the edge and hold her there until she was begging—so desperate for my cock she wouldn't notice the pain.

My hand slid down her body, pushing her shorts and panties down before I slipped a finger inside her. Christ, she was tight. Wet. Perfect. I moaned, my cock aching as I added another finger, stretching her gently. Her body tensed and fluttered around me, and I fought to keep my control. I kept my fingers buried deep and circled her clit with my thumb, coaxing her open, listening to the breathless sounds she made.

Her hips jerked into my hand, and she started to come apart, her moans turning frantic.

I wanted to feel her come again. I needed her relaxed, melted, ready to take me.

My pace quickened—deeper, harder—until she shattered, her body arching and clenching around my fingers. The hot, tight squeeze nearly undid me.

I waited until she was soft and pliant before pulling free, fumbling with my jeans, too far gone to slow down now. I kicked them off, my cock springing free, painfully hard. Her eyes widened.

"Clay," she whispered. "You're... big."

I let out a rough laugh. "I'll be gentle," I promised, settling between her legs.

I grabbed the condom from my back pocket, tore it open, and rolled it on with shaking hands. I was so fucking ready. So desperate to make her mine.

"Okay?" I asked.

She nodded, breathless.

I pressed the head of my cock to her slick pussy and eased in, just the tip, just enough to feel her heat.

I nearly lost it.

"Oh my god," she breathed.

I froze, straining to hold still.

"Okay?" I asked again.

"It's... a lot," she whispered.

"We can stop."

"No," she said quickly. "I want this. I want you."

I groaned, pushing in deeper, feeling her stretch around me, tight and hot and so goddamn perfect. Inch by inch, I filled her, holding back everything in me that wanted to move.

She pulsed around me, and I held still, letting her adjust.

"Fuck, Eliza," I whispered. "You're amazing."

Her hands gripped my back, her body trembling, but not pulling away. Her hips lifted, urging me deeper, and I lost a little more control.

Still, I went slow. Careful. Watching her.

And then—

"Clay, I'm not glass. I won't break." Her voice was thick with need. "Fuck me. Now. I need all of you."

I let out a groan that bordered on a growl, every muscle in me coiled and ready to snap.

I brought my thumb to her clit, circling softly, waiting for that final shift in her body. The moment she fully let go.

And then I pulled back and drove into her, breaking through her barrier with one deep thrust.

She gasped—a sharp intake of breath—but then, "Yes, Clay. Yes."

Her legs locked around me, her hips rising to meet mine. "Don't stop."

She was slick and hot and unbelievably tight. I thrust again, watching her face, reading every breath, every twitch, until I knew she was okay.

And then I gave in to it.

The rhythm built—hard, fast, the bed creaking beneath us. Her moans, her gasps, her body wrapped around mine... it was everything.

"Clay, I—" She didn't finish. Just arched, her body going taut as she came, her pussy clenching around me, pulling me with her.

I came hard, shuddering, my hips jerking as the pleasure tore through me. It was like nothing I'd ever felt—hot, raw, consuming.

I stayed inside her, holding her close, letting our bodies unwind together. Her chest pressed to mine, her breath soft against my neck.

I didn't move. Didn't want to.

Eliza was mine.

I didn't know if I believed in love. But if this wasn't it... I didn't know what else could be.

I rolled us gently, keeping her close. My skin was damp, my heart still racing.

She made a slight, sleepy sound and burrowed into me.

Fuck, she was perfect.

And I was the luckiest man alive.

I knew it wouldn't be easy. I'd screw up again. I'd have to prove myself to her, to everyone who thought I wasn't good enough.

But right now, none of that mattered.

Not the town. Not the past.

Just her.

"Eliza," I whispered, holding her tighter. "I'm not going anywhere. I'm not—"

But she was already asleep.

Already safe.

Already mine.

Chapter Nine

ELIZA

I woke to loud, insistent banging on the door. My body was still loose and tender, barely wrapped in the sheet. Clay was beside me, warm and solid, his arm draped over my waist.

"Someone's here," I murmured, still half-asleep.

He groaned, low and lazy. "Ignore it."

The knocking came again, louder this time.

"Maybe it's important?" I whispered.

Clay sighed and rolled out of bed, tugging on his jeans but skipping the shirt. He ran a hand through his hair, then gave me a long, lingering look like he was seriously considering climbing back in.

"I'll get it," he said.

I watched him walk away—barefoot, bare-chested, every muscle shifting under his skin. He opened the door, blocking the view with his body.

And then I heard the voice.

Familiar. Annoyed.

"Holy shit, Clay Walker."

Lola.

Panic surged. I scrambled for clothes, yanking on a tank top and panties, then grabbed the sheet and wrapped it around me like a toga, as if that might help.

I rounded the corner just in time to see Lola storm past Clay like a woman on a mission.

A very loud, very terrifying mission.

"I swear to God," she snapped, eyes blazing, "if you so much as messed up one hair on her head, I'll cut your brake lines and sleep like a baby."

Tanner followed, looking marginally apologetic. "I told her it might not be necessary—"

"You told me he hurt her," Lola hissed, spinning on him.

"Inadvertently!" Tanner shot back. "That's what he said. He inadvertently hurt her."

Lola turned back to Clay, who stood tall in my doorway, jaw tight, hands relaxed.

"Lola," I said, stepping into view, the sheet clutched around me like I was auditioning for a low-budget film.

Three heads swiveled toward me.

Clay's expression softened.

Lola's narrowed. "Are you kidding me right now?"

"I'm fine," I said quickly. "Everything's fine."

She looked between us, and my cheeks flushed.

"Oh my God," she muttered. "You're glowing. You're literally glowing." Her voice pitched into something between horror and awe. "I'm going to kill him and then bleach my eyeballs."

"Lola," Tanner said gently, "maybe we should—"

"I told you," she snapped. "Big. Broody. Trouble."

"I'm not trouble," Clay said, calm but firm. "And I'm not going to let you talk about me like I'm not standing here."

That stopped her.

"I care about your sister. I fucked up—yeah. But I fixed it. Or I'm trying to. And I'm not walking away."

Lola opened her mouth. Then closed it.

I stepped in. "I appreciate the concern. I do. But I'm okay. Clay didn't hurt me."

She turned to me, arms crossed. "Then why did Tanner say—"

"Because I freaked out," I admitted. "I got scared. Misread something. Clay came after me. He explained. And now... we're here."

Lola stared. Then sighed and brushed invisible lint from her jacket.

"Well," she said. "If you hurt her again, I'm not kidding about the brake lines."

Clay nodded. "Understood."

Tanner looked at both of us. "I need a drink."

They didn't stay long. Tanner managed to herd Lola out the door with a muttered, "Let's go before she actually follows through on the bleach thing."

Lola glared over her shoulder. "This isn't over."

Then they were gone.

The apartment was quiet again.

Too quiet.

I turned slowly, still swaddled in the sheet, and found Clay watching me.

Not guilty. Not cautious.

Just... watching.

"Sorry about that," I said, exhaling. "My sisters are very... invested."

He raised an eyebrow. "That was invested?"

I blinked.

He shrugged. "I was expecting weapons."

A surprised laugh bubbled out of me, breaking the tension.

He stepped forward and tucked a piece of hair behind my ear, his thumb grazing my cheek.

"You okay?" he asked.

I nodded. "Yeah. I think so."

His gaze held mine.

Then, just barely, he smiled. "Glowing, huh?"

I rolled my eyes. "Shut up."

"Make me," he murmured, and his mouth found mine.

His hands slipped under the sheet, pulling me in, the world falling away as he kissed me deeper. I tugged him toward the bedroom, not holding anything back.

He kicked off his jeans, and we tumbled into the bed—a tangle of limbs, laughter, and raw, desperate need. I straddled him, thighs braced on either side of his hips, hands flat against his chest.

For the first time, I felt in control.

His cock was hard beneath me, thick and hot, and I ground against him, both of us groaning at the contact.

He reached between us, his fingers teasing my clit, driving me wild.

"Clay," I gasped, hips rocking.

The pressure built fast, sweet, and electric.

I reached down, wrapping my hand around him, stroking slow and sure. He jerked into my grip, groaning.

"Clay," I panted. "Do you have another condom?"

His eyes darkened. "Fuck, yes. In my pants."

I reached down and grabbed one, handing it to him. He tore it open with shaking hands and rolled it on quickly.

Then Clay sat up, pulling me close, his mouth hot on my breast. I gasped, arching into him, guiding his cock to my entrance.

"Are you ready for this, sweetheart?" he asked.

"Yes," I breathed. "I'm ready."

I sank down onto him slowly, gasping as he stretched and filled me. So deep. So full. It was almost too much. And exactly right.

I rocked my hips, the pressure exquisite. He groaned, his hands tight on my waist. "Fuck, Eliza. Take me. Take it all."

I did.

I took everything. And it was glorious.

He sucked one nipple into his mouth, his fingers pinching and teasing the other, and I was gone—wild and wet and clenching around him.

I reached between us, stroked my clit, desperate and bold.

"Fuck, Eliza," he growled. "That's the sexiest thing I've ever seen. Take it, baby. Take your pleasure."

He thrust up into me, deep and hard.

"I want to watch you come."

His words undid me.

I stroked my clit faster, desperate, frantic, and rode him hard, slamming down on his cock as he rose up to meet me.

The orgasm hit hard. Sudden and blinding. My body trembled, clenching around him, my cry loud and raw.

Clay cursed and followed, his release crashing into mine, his body jerking and throbbing, his arms locking around me.

We shook together.

Shuddered together.

And when it was over, we stayed sweaty, breathless, tangled.

Whole.

It was everything.

Epilogue

ELIZA

S ix months later...

It was the kind of day that made Briar Hill feel like a storybook.

Blue sky. Soft breeze. Not a single glitter spill in sight. We'd claimed a grassy corner of the park with too many blankets, three coolers, and enough Thorne sister energy to make the ducks rethink their life choices.

Clay was at the grill, flipping burgers with his usual quiet focus. Simon and Tanner were deep in a debate over charcoal versus gas, complete with historical references (Simon) and profanity (Tanner). Dean stood nearby, arms crossed, offering one word of input every five minutes, still winning the argument.

Veronica had already vetoed the disposable cutlery.

"I brought real forks," she said, unfolding linen napkins like classified documents. "Because I have standards."

"I brought wine," said Vivian, lifting a bottle from a sequined tote. "Because I don't."

Lola rolled her eyes. "Where's Eliza?"

"I'm here!" I called, holding up a canvas tote.

Three heads turned. Four, if you counted Dean's subtle but very alert glance.

"That's the surprise activity voice," Vivian muttered. "I *hate* the surprise activity voice."

I turned on my best Eliza smile and knelt beside the blanket, pulling out a stack of soft cotton t-shirts. "I made picnic shirts!"

All three of them groaned in unison.

"I swear," Lola said, "if mine says something like *Sunshine Sister*, I'm drinking the citronella."

"It doesn't," I promised, passing them out. "Just try them on."

Veronica glanced down and smiled: *Best Aunt Ever.*

Lola unfolded hers next: *Promoted to Aunt.*

Vivian blinked at hers: *Aunt-in-Training.*

Three sets of eyes flicked to me in perfect unison.

I pulled out the last shirt—blush pink, folded with care: *Baby Thorne-Walker Coming Soon.*

Veronica gasped. Vivian screamed. Lola tackled me with a hug that nearly knocked the breath out of me.

"You're serious?" she whispered, already tearing up.

I nodded, barely able to speak. "We are."

Clay stepped up behind me, one hand settling gently over my stomach.

Veronica kissed my cheek. Vivian blinked hard and fanned her face. "Okay, well now I'm emotional *and* furious. Why didn't you give us a waterproof mascara warning?"

Lola swore under her breath and hugged me tighter.

And just when the noise began to settle, Vivian leaned back and looked at her shirt again.

"Wait," she sniffed. "Why does mine say *in training?*"

I shrugged. "Felt accurate."

Vivian turned to Veronica. "Yours doesn't say *in training.*"

Veronica just sipped her wine. "Doesn't need to."

Later, when the grill had cooled and the sun dipped behind the trees, I curled up beside Clay on the picnic blanket, full and flushed with too many emotions to name.

Tanner was helping Lola stake down their blanket after a gust of wind tried to take it out like a parachute—his expression all focus, hers all fire. Vivian had hijacked the Bluetooth speaker and was coaching Dean through a slow shimmy. He looked pained. She looked delighted. Veronica and Simon sat side by side on a quilt, pretending to read—but mostly stealing kisses when they thought no one was looking.

Clay laced his fingers with mine.

"You're glowing," he said softly.

I laughed. "Still?"

"Always."

I leaned my head on his shoulder, his heartbeat steady beneath my cheek.

And for the first time in a long time, I felt like every part of me, the sweet, the silly, the soft, was not just seen but celebrated.

***

Dear Reader,

Thank you so much for reading *Lessons & Leather*! I hope Eliza and Clay's story wrapped around your heart the same way it wrapped around mine—quietly at first, then all at once.

This book was a love letter to softness and strength, to unexpected chemistry, and to the kind of tenderness that makes you feel safe enough to fall apart—and bold enough to fall in love. Watching Eliza step into her own power, and Clay learn to believe he was worthy of hers, was one of the most emotional journeys I've written.

If their story made you smile, swoon, or even tear up just a little—I'd be so grateful if you left a review. Every single one helps readers find the Thorne Sisters and makes it possible for me to keep telling stories like this one. You can review the book on Amazon here.

Thank you for spending time in Briar Hill. And if you've read the whole Thorne Sisters series, I hope you know by now—whatever kind of woman you are, you are not too much. You are not not enough. You are just right.

With love,

Hana York

***

Hana York Books

Hearts on Duty Series

Sparks of Temptation

Love's Anchor

On Call for You

Investigating Desire

Falling for the Rescue

A Heart Worth Mending

***

Falling for the Billionaire Series

Hating Mr. Wentworth

Tempting Mr. Dawson
Unraveling Mr. Ashford

***

The Thorne Sisters Series

Ink & Iron
Silk & Silence
Pleasure & Prose
Lessons & Leather

***

For a full list of titles, please visit Hana York's website
www.HanaYork.com

About the Author

Hana York writes fast-paced, heart-pounding contemporary romance packed with irresistible heroes, strong heroines, laugh-out-loud banter, and just the right amount of spice to keep things sizzling. Her books are for readers who love grumpy men falling hard, fierce women who don't need saving, and the kind of chemistry that sparks off the page.

When she's not crafting stories full of love, tension, and toe-curling moments, you'll find her daydreaming about small-town charm, plotting ridiculous meet-cutes, and consuming an unhealthy amount of coffee. She believes in happily-ever-afters, overprotective heroes who don't stand a chance against their heroines, and that every great love story should come with a side of sass.

If you love forced proximity, off-limits attraction, sizzling tension, and romance that makes your heart race, welcome to the world of Hana York!

Follow Hana York for new releases, exclusive content, and behind-the-scenes fun! www.HanaYork.com

Find all her books here: https://www.amazon.com/author/hanayork

Follow her on Instagram: https://www.instagram.com/hanayorkromance/

Follow her on Facebook: https://www.facebook.com/hanayorkromance/

Follow her on Good Reads: https://www.goodreads.com/author/show/54826946.Hana_York

Join her mailing list here: https://www.hanayork.com/subscribe

More to Read

I f you enjoyed this story, I've got more where that came from! Keep reading for a look at my other books.

Hearts on Duty Series

Sparks of Temptation

A sizzling small-town romance where forced proximity turns up the heat between a stubborn chef and a protective firefighter.

Olivia Harper came to Anchor Bay for a fresh start—not a flirty distraction. After rebuilding her life, she has no time for complications, especially the kind that come with broad shoulders, a cocky grin, and a hero complex.

Jack Lawson knows how to keep his cool under pressure. As a firefighter, protecting people is second nature. But Olivia? She doesn't want rescuing, and she sure as hell doesn't want him getting too close. When a plumbing mishap lands him as her unexpected housemate, their battle of wills turns into something neither of them can ignore.

The problem? Olivia has spent years proving she doesn't need anyone, while Jack's instincts tell him to stand back before he wants something he can't have. But some flames refuse to die out...**A small town full of charm. A slow-burn romance packed with heat. A love story that proves the best things in life are worth the risk.**

***

Love's Anchor

A sizzling small-town romance where years of friendship ignite into something neither of them can ignore.

Brooke Taylor has spent years keeping her feelings for Theo Morgan buried beneath sharp comebacks and stubborn denial. As a no-nonsense cop in Anchor Bay, she's never let emotions get in the way of the job—especially when it comes to the charming, frustrating bar owner who knows exactly how to push her buttons.

Theo has always played it safe when it comes to Brooke. She's his best friend, his steady constant—the one woman he can't afford to lose. But when a break-in at his bar forces them into close quarters, the tension between them finally boils over.

Can they risk their friendship to take a chance on love? Or will fear keep them apart forever?**A small town full of charm. A slow-burn romance packed with heat. A love story where friendship is just the beginning.**

***

On Call for You

He swore she was off-limits. She's ready to prove him wrong.

Dr. Sophie Whitaker has spent her career proving herself in a world that underestimates her. As a brilliant but petite doctor, she's fought for respect every step of the way. Moving back to Anchor Bay is supposed to be a fresh start—not a temptation in the form of Lucas Carter. The rugged EMT with a cocky grin and a hero complex. The man her brother trusts with his life... and the one she should definitely stay away from.

Lucas Carter lives by two rules: stay cool under pressure and never, ever cross the line with Sophie Whitaker. Even if she's gorgeous. Even if she's sharp-witted and impossible to ignore. Even if, after one stormy encounter stranded together, the idea of walking away feels damn near impossible.

Now, every stolen glance and lingering touch has Lucas questioning everything—especially the rule that's kept him from going after the one woman he can't stop thinking about. Falling for Sophie could mean risking his oldest friendship. But walking away? That might be the biggest mistake of his life.

A sizzling, forbidden love, best friend's little sister romance packed with tension, heat, and undeniable chemistry!

***

Investigating Desire

A Slow-Burn Romantic Suspense with a Grumpy Detective and the Journalist Who Won't Back Down

Detective Nate Whitaker has sworn off love. After a messy divorce, he's buried himself in his work, content to keep his emotions locked away. But when a bold, relentless journalist starts shadowing him for an exclusive story, their push-and-pull dynamic ignites a slow burn neither of them can ignore.

Tessa Donovan has worked hard to make a name for herself. She's determined to crack open a case that's rocked this small town, even if it means getting under the skin of a brooding detective who wants nothing to do with her. But when her investigation stirs up danger, Nate has no choice but to keep her close. What starts as a reluctant partnership turns into something far more dangerous—a fiery attraction neither of them is ready for.

With a growing threat looming and tension crackling between them, this small-town romantic suspense is about to heat up. Can Nate and Tessa untangle the case before it's too late, or will their undeniable chemistry turn into the biggest risk of all?

***

Falling for the Rescue

A Forced Proximity, Search and Rescue Romance Packed with Heat, Heart, and High Stakes

Ryan Anderson thrives in the chaos of Search and Rescue, risking everything to save those in danger. He's fiercely independent, highly skilled, and never the one needing help—until a treacherous storm and a botched rescue mission leave him stranded, injured, and facing the one situation he can't control.

Enter Sam Monroe—a tough, no-nonsense ex-military K9 handler who's spent years proving she doesn't need anyone. Haunted by her past and more comfortable in survival mode than emotional entanglements, Sam doesn't have time for distractions—especially not the kind with broad shoulders, smoldering intensity, and a stubborn streak to match her own.

Forced to wait out the storm in a remote cabin in the wilderness, their reluctant alliance turns into something far more dangerous. Tensions ignite. Sparks fly. But neither of them is built for surrender—especially when old wounds and hidden vulnerabilities threaten to unravel the fragile trust between them.

Will Sam and Ryan let down their walls and take a risk on love? Or will fear and pride keep them from the one person who finally sees them for who they truly are?

***

A Heart Worth Mending

Penelope Everett is chaos wrapped in sunshine and cinnamon. Milo Turner is a brooding small-town vet who prefers his solitude—and his scars—untouched.

But when an injured fox, a runaway goat, and a perfectly imperfect dance in a flour-dusted kitchen spark something real, Milo and Penelope are forced to face the truth: love isn't always neat. It's messy. It's brave. It's terrifying.

And sometimes... it's exactly what you need to heal.

Can a woman learning to choose herself risk everything on a man still learning how to stay?**A Heart Worth Mending is a small-town, age-gap romance packed with heart, heat, and a hero worth waiting for. Perfect for fans of grumpy-sunshine pairings, emotionally satisfying slow burns, and heroines who never stop believing in love—even when it hurts.**

Falling for the Billionaire Series

Hating Mr. Wentworth

They're supposed to be enemies—so why does arguing feel like foreplay?

Liz Bentley built her career on grit, caffeine, and a zero-tolerance policy for entitled men—especially not the newly appointed CEO with a famous last name and a face straight off a magazine cover. Brett Wentworth might be rich, polished, and maddeningly smug, but Liz knows his type: privilege, power, and betrayal wrapped in a designer suit.

Brett didn't ask to inherit the mess his father made of Bright Spark. But the moment Liz storms into his boardroom—all fire, wit, and defiance—he knows two things: she's the sharpest mind in the company... and the one woman he shouldn't want.

Their arguments are electric. Their chemistry, impossible to ignore. And one dangerously hot encounter changes everything. Now Brett has one shot to prove he's nothing like the men who came before—and everything Liz never saw coming.

Enemies on paper. Fireworks in person. A hot, hilarious romance that's one HR violation away from disaster—or the most delicious kind of downfall.

***

Tempting Mr. Dawson

A sizzling, laugh-out-loud billionaire romcom about mistaken identity, forbidden chemistry, and the hidden moment that might just lead to love.

Travel writer Piper Winslow is in paradise—but she's not here to relax. Her assignment? Review Coral Bay Resort and keep things strictly professional. But the guy in the Hawaiian shirt who offers her a "real" tour of the property? He's messing with her objectivity—and tempting her to break all her rules.

Logan Dawson didn't mean to lie. When Piper mistakes him for a charming staff member instead of the CEO of the luxury resort she's reviewing, he doesn't correct her. For once, someone sees him, not his title. And walking away from that? Not so easy.

What starts as playful banter turns into an afternoon of unforgettable heat in a hidden grotto. But when the truth comes out, so does the fallout. Now Logan has to prove that the man she fell for is the real him—and that what sparked between them wasn't just a vacation fling.

Tempting Mr. Dawson is a steamy billionaire rom-com with sharp banter, tropical heat, mistaken identities, and a CEO who'll risk everything to win back the woman who saw through him.

***

Unraveling Mr. Ashford

Mia Wilder is a glitter bomb of chaos, creativity, and caffeine—and even she knows it's time for a vacation when her vision board catches fire. (Literally.)

So when a family friend pulls strings to score her a solo escape to a luxury island resort, Mia says yes—because nothing says self-care like seven days of sunshine, silence, and SPF 50.

Thanks to a booking snafu—and a storm that knocks out all communication—Mia finds herself stranded with Grant Ashford, a brooding tech billionaire who clearly didn't plan on sharing his R&R with an overcaffeinated sunbeam who narrates her inner monologue like it's a podcast.

He's grumpy, guarded, and allergic to distractions. She's sunshine in designer flip-flops. And neither of them is prepared for what happens next.

The Thorne Sisters Series

Ink & Iron

A grumpy, guarded veteran. A tattoo artist who turns pain into beauty. When trust feels like temptation, survival won't be enough.

Tanner Maddox didn't come to Briar Hill looking for second chances. He came to outrun the past, bury the guilt, and forget the wreckage he left behind. But one step into Needle & Ink—and one sharp-eyed artist who turns scars into stories—shatters every line he swore he wouldn't cross.

Lola Thorne knows better than to get tangled in someone else's broken pieces. She's got a tattoo shop to run, a past she won't talk about, and one rule she never breaks: don't fall for clients. Especially not a brooding ex-soldier with hands built for violence and a gaze that feels like a promise she can't afford to believe.

The tattoo was supposed to be just a cover. Instead, it uncovers the one thing neither of them thought they deserved: a future. He's all muscle, silence, and pain. She's all sharp edges, rough laughter, and a heart stitched together with ink and stubbornness. Together, they're something neither of them expected—and everything they didn't know how to want.

Walls will crumble. Rules will shatter. And when it's all stripped bare, the only thing left will be the truth—and the fight for a love worth every scar.

Ink & Iron is a steamy, emotional small-town romance about a grumpy veteran, a fierce tattoo artist, slow-burn tension, off-the-charts chemistry, and love so raw it leaves a mark deeper than skin.

***

Silk & Silence

She's built her world on control. He's forgotten what it means to want. But some sparks don't ask permission before they burn.

Vivian Thorne built her life on polish, power, and impeccable control. As the owner of the Velvet Room—a high-end burlesque club known for its vintage glamours—she knows how to captivate a crowd without ever letting anyone close. Love is a liability she can't afford—and perfection is the armor she never removes.

Dean Thatcher is a gruff, guarded divorce attorney who's seen every way love can break, bleed, and betray. He doesn't do risks. He doesn't do chaos. And he sure as hell doesn't fall for women who look like trouble wrapped in red lipstick and secrets.

Their connection should have been a brief spark—an impulse easy to ignore. But the more Dean uncovers the woman beneath the polish, the more he realizes she's the most dangerously real thing he's ever craved. And the more Vivian lets him in, the more terrified she is that he'll walk away when he sees the cracks no amount of armor can hide. Masks will slip. Hearts will break open. And when survival isn't enough anymore, they'll have to risk everything—for a love that strips them bare.

Silk & Silence is a steamy, emotional small-town romance about fierce vulnerability, slow-burn passion, and love without conditions. Perfect for fans of broken heroes, scarred heroines, emotional healing, and off-the-charts chemistry.

***

Pleasure & Prose

She's pure confidence and provocation. He's all restraint and repressed desire. But when opposites combust, even the rules don't stand a chance.

Simon Radcliffe is a buttoned-up British professor teaching at the local university, all nervous smiles and devastatingly proper manners. But when a wrong turn leads him through the doors of Pleasure & Co., he meets Veronica Thorne—a woman who exudes power, mystery, and the kind of sensual self-possession that makes him forget how to breathe.

Veronica doesn't do flustered. And she definitely doesn't go for repressed academics. But there's something about Simon—something curious and unguarded—that makes her pause. And when he asks her to tea—with the stiff sincerity of a man completely out of his depth—she says yes. Against every instinct, she says yes.

What begins as a slow, simmering pull becomes a wild-fire neither of them is ready for. And when the past rears its nosy, unwelcome head, they'll have to decide what they're really fighting for.

Pleasure & Prose is a steamy, emotional small-town romance about opposites that ignite, slow burns that explode, and a cinnamon roll hero who learns the right woman doesn't just unravel you—she shows you who you've been all along.

***

Lessons & Leather

She's never been touched. He's never been trusted. But when a sunshine schoolteacher crashes into a broody mechanic—literally—the sparks don't stop flying.

Eliza Thorne has spent her whole life being good. Good daughter. Good sister. Good teacher. She keeps the peace, keeps things running, and keeps her deepest desires tucked safely out of sight. Wanting more has never felt like an option—until a fender bender introduces her to Clay Walker, the town's broodiest mechanic with a jaw that could cut glass and eyes that see far too much.

Clay doesn't do soft. Doesn't do complications. He keeps his head down, runs his garage, and avoids anything that might crack the armor he's spent years building. But Eliza Thorne—sunshine smile, cherry earrings, and quiet strength—doesn't just crack his walls. She dismantles them.

Their connection is electric. Impossible. Inevitable. But if they want more than just heat, they'll have to believe something neither of them has ever been told—that real love doesn't just hold space—it makes you feel like you belong in it.

Lessons & Leather is a steamy, small-town opposites-attract romance between a woman learning to want and a man learning he's wanted. Featuring emotional firsts, protective tension, and the kind of slow burn that scorches when it finally ignites.

***

To stay up to date on all of my releases, subscribe to my mailing list here!

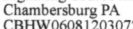